‖‖‖ ‖‖‖‖‖‖‖‖‖ ‖ ‖‖ ‖‖‖‖‖‖‖‖‖‖‖‖‖‖‖
◁ **W9-AXQ-859**

FROM OUT OF THE DARKNESS ...

It was sometime between 9:00 and 10:00 P.M. when the first witness spotted the gargantuan craft moving almost directly overhead. A group of some twenty residents collected on the main street to view the extraordinary spectacle. Foreboding and ominous, the great bulk of the craft just hung there. There were absolutely no engine sounds. The light from the object was intense enough to reflect from rooftops and cast an eerie phosphorescent glow across most of the town. Dogs began to howl in the streets.

"It was like we were being watched," recalls Ceballos's Mayor Silva. "After two or three minutes of this, people became very worried. They felt panic. This was a very frightening experience."

Other Avon Books of Similar Interest

THE BERMUDA TRIANGLE
by Charles Berlitz

EDGAR CAYCE SPEAKS
edited by Brett Bolton

THE EARTH CHRONICLES
by Zecharia Sitchin

STAIRWAY TO HEAVEN
THE 12TH PLANET
THE WARS OF GODS AND MEN

Avon Books are available at special quantity discounts for bulk purchases for sales promotions, premiums, fund raising or educational use. Special books, or book excerpts, can also be created to fit specific needs.

For details write or telephone the office of the Director of Special Markets, Avon Books, Dept. FP, 1790 Broadway, New York, New York 10019, 212-399-1357.

THE ZONE OF SILENCE

GERRY HUNT

In collaboration with
Professor Harry de la Pena

AVON
PUBLISHERS OF BARD, CAMELOT, DISCUS AND FLARE BOOKS

to

Luis Maeda, M.D.
a true samurai explorer

and for

Mickey and Sean
with love

THE ZONE OF SILENCE is an original publication of Avon Books.
This work has never before appeared in book form.

AVON BOOKS
A division of
The Hearst Corporation
1790 Broadway
New York, New York 10019

Copyright © 1986 by Gerry Hunt
Published by arrangement with the author
Library of Congress Catalog Card Number: 86-90905
ISBN: 0-380-89806-3

All rights reserved, which includes the right to reproduce this book or
portions thereof in any form whatsoever except as provided by the U.S.
Copyright Law. For information address Adele Leone Literary Agency,
Inc., 26 Nantucket Place, Scarsdale, New York 10583.

First Avon Printing: December 1986

AVON TRADEMARK REG. U.S. PAT. OFF. AND IN OTHER COUNTRIES, MARCA
REGISTRADA, HECHO EN U.S.A.

Printed in the U.S.A.

K–R   10   9   8   7   6   5   4   3   2   1

CONTENTS

ACKNOWLEDGMENTS

The author would like to acknowledge the following people for their invaluable help and assistance in pulling together this book:

John Blosser, an astute reporter and friend; Miguel Angel Ruelas Talamantes, general manager of *El Siglo de Torreon;* Francisco Fernandez Torres, Chief of the Department of Cultural Affairs, County of Torreon; Vivi de la Pena; Isabel Sifuentes and Amparo Sifuentes Luna for their communications skills; Generoso Pope, Jr., who knows why; and Tom Hopkinson, who started the whole ball rolling.

Thanks also to Bernard Simms of Picture Perfect Express, Danbury, Connecticut, for his photographic expertise; Bob Frazer for the use of his darkroom facilities; and Chuck's Steak House of Danbury for being there.

This book would not have been possible without the unswerving support and patience of its editor, John Douglas of Avon, and my intrepid agents and friends, Adele Leone and Richard Monaco.

A very special thanks to Rosendo Aguilera for revealing so much; to Dr. Sergio Flores y Nava for being a scientific companion and explaining so much, and his wonderful wife, Mia Lewis Flores, for translating and supporting so much.

And appreciations to Pudsey, who, despite being able to neither read nor write, was instrumental in great chunks of the original manuscript.

This book would hardly have been possible without the great friendship and guidance of Harry de la Pena, ''father'' of the Zone of Silence.

Preface

The Sky Is Falling

THE END OF the universe came to the terrified inhabitants of a small, dusty corner of the North American continent on February 8, 1969, at precisely 1:05 A.M.

In a blinding flash the cobalt coldness of the desert night sky was ablaze with a stratospheric likeness to the flare of pure sodium; a brilliance of such intensity that night was instantly transformed to day.

A gigantic white-hot fire sphere was descending from the heavens, displaying the clarity of a dozen suns. The purifying vision rocketed out of the northwest, screaming in a wide arc toward the southeast.

It had already left a legacy of scorched sky across Arizona, New Mexico, and Texas. And now the awesome apparition was heading for the tiny ramshackle dirt town of Ceballos, where meteorites incredibly fall like rain. The desert-hardened, swarthy-skinned inhabitants of this arid Mexican outpost treat the daily meteorite showers with respect—but never with the awe they were feeling now.

First a rolling of low rumbles, and then alarming screech-

1

ing and hissing sounds, brought the natives nervously to the doorways of their adobe shacks.

A furious white-blue peacock tail, superheated fusion in the thin atmosphere, fanned out across the heavens. And what was mere seconds in real time was taking an eternity to digest in the minds of unbelieving humans shielding their eyes to peer upward.

For Maria Sanchez, in Ceballos, it was surely the end of the world. She fell to her knees, repeatedly blessing herself. A crucifix hanging loosely on a chain now embedded itself painfully in her sternum as she hugged two terrified infants to her chest in the paralyzed clutch of a mother in despair. Miguel Sanchez, slightly behind her, placed his shaking hand on his wife's shoulder and began in a quavering voice to recite the Hail Mary.

Jesus Ortago rushed from his nearby adobe, saw the sky falling, and began to weep openly, arms outstretched, in the center of the town's dirt-paved main street.

Others in Ceballos soon followed to witness the celestial spectacle. Many of them prostrated their bodies on the ground and made final acts of contrition.

The atmosphere in Chihuahua City, 125 miles away, was, for the moment, less intense.

Newspaper editor Guillermo Asunsolo strolled unwillingly to the outside of Chihuahua City's *El Heraldo* offices despite the urgent cries from a hysterical night watchman. He had no idea that what he was about to witness in the distant sky would turn the printer's ink in his blood ice cold.

On first impression as he stared upward, his mind drew a complete blank. Shooting stars he'd seen. This was something entirely different. He remembers thinking at the time that it was rather childish and strange for words like "cataclysmic" to keep running through the head of a hard-nosed professional newsman who'd seen it all, many times over.

Back in the direction of the descending phenomenon, at Pueblito de Allende, a small village near Ceballos and some twenty miles east of the city of Hidalgo del Parral, there were no frightening streams of pyrotechnics, no mesmerizing trails of vividness across the night—the whole entire visible universe, every centimeter of it from one horizon to the other, suddenly ignited with a blinding fury.

One description, related later to a photographer, was, "It was like looking straight into your flash camera—but much, much more powerful."

There was absolutely no warning in Pueblito de Allende. And there was good reason for this. The town was at the epicenter, almost directly underneath the cosmic fireball.

Some village folk remember unearthly sounds seconds before the sky exploded.

"I heard the noises—they awoke me. It was dark and I ran outside," recalled Alvarez de Carrillo. "I could hear nothing but strange crackling, sizzling sounds. Sounds like a pig roasting on a spit.

"I looked up and I could see nothing unusual in the sky. Then, very suddenly, the whole sky exploded in a brilliant white light. Everything was like the brightest daylight for a second or so. I had to shield my eyes, it was very painful. It was all over in an instant.

"I thought a bomb had dropped, but for a moment I heard no sound at all."

There was no time for hysteria in Pueblito de Allende, near to the center of impact; it was all over before even the swiftest mind could comprehend.

A shock wave followed immediately.

An earsplitting whiplash crack electrified the air, and instantaneously the world somersaulted with a thunderclap that wasn't only heard but also felt as a dull pain deep in the bowels. The ground trembled, erupted, and set back down in a deafening roar of outraged agony.

Then—nothing! Just the sounds of men, women, and children weeping.

The greatest meteorite to hit the world in modern times had struck. It was to be called Allende.

A space nomad, bigger than ever before, had found its last resting place . . . in the Zone of Silence.

Whatever science theorizes about the Big Bang and the origins of the universe, there was no doubt this small part of Mexico, home to the strange area known as the Zone of Silence, had just become the terrestrial final residence of one of creation's wayward children.

Conceived in the explosion that spawned all, the Allende meteorite had been hurled to the edges of the universe. And on its lonely voyage the meteorite had crossed light-years of space, unhindered since the beginnings of time.

Before one single-celled animal evolved in the primordial soup, Allende was heading toward the Zone. It was still on course when prehistoric dinosaurs roamed; as man first burned his hands with fire; when Babylon was a plant nursery; as a British king broke his quill on the Magna Carta; when scientists still believed the world was square, and Christopher Columbus stumbled on the Americas. Allende's course, as straight as an intergalactic arrow, never varied.

Allende was always predestined to hit one exact spot on Earth: the Zone of Silence.

It might have looked like the end of the world to some, but the fact was that the end of the universe had come to the Zone.

Millions of meteorites are unexplainably attracted to the Zone, but Allende was without doubt the king. As unique and important as the Allende meteorite has become to scientists and physicists, it is, however, just a small part of an intriguingly bizarre jigsaw puzzle that makes up one of the strangest places on Planet Earth.

Welcome to the Zone of Silence!

Introduction

ON A BLISTERING desert day in the mid-sixties, "The Luminous One" made the first dramatic discoveries which would confirm the existence of the Zone of Silence.

Although tales and legends abound from the parched area where the Mexican states of Chihuahua, Coahuila, and Durango come together in a triangle, nobody had ever provided any concrete proof that strange phenomena did exist there.

Bizarre red cacti, purple desert trees, mutant animals, strange magnetic anomalies, myriads of unearthly lights and gigantic UFOs, were all reported from the inhospitable desert.

But it wasn't until the Luminous One made contact with the Zone that people started taking the fables seriously.

El Luminero—The Luminous One—is Professor Harry de la Pena, an engineer and academic, graduate of Paris's famous Sorbonne, and at that time a researcher in organic chemistry at the Instituto Technologico de Laguna in Torreon, the largest city near the Zone of Silence.

Blue-eyed, and with the palest of complexions, de la

Pena had been given the nickname El Luminero back in his college days when the handsome blond-haired Mexican—who for all the world could have been descended from the elite of Aryan stock—stood out from his fellow swarthy, dark-skinned students.

The nickname stuck, and now, some two decades after his studies had taken him from Mexico to Paris's prestigious Sorbonne, the University of Koln in Germany, and then nuclear physics labs in England, Holland, Belgium, Italy, Austria, and Czechoslovakia, and the University of California at Riverside, the Luminous One was to make his greatest discovery—the bizarre Zone of Silence

There was no doubt about de la Pena's academic brilliance; but more than anything, after his worldwide scientific travels, he had an unswerving curiosity to probe the unknown.

What de la Pena didn't know on that scorching Saturday in 1966, as he and a party of friends set out from Torreon, was that an innocent photographic expedition was to turn a world of science fiction into science fact.

The Luminous One was to become the father of the Zone of Silence.

Secrecy

The Zone was dubbed with its bizarre name for good reason—radio waves disappear and all communications are suddenly and inexplicably lost in parts of this mysterious area.

In the Zone you are literally very much alone; strange unexplained forces hold you prisoner with a barrier of silence against the outside world. Once inside the Zone you could be in the remotest spot on the planet.

But if that weren't enough, the Zone of Silence also hides a mind-boggling nightmare world of bizarre animals, plants, and strange phenomena. It is a place where the laws of nature are twisted and warped by unseen forces that have defied logical explanation by even the most eminent of scientists.

For years this mysterious place was a closely guarded secret.

While investigators of the paranormal and unexplained have reported on such global oddities as the Bermuda Triangle, Japan's Devil's Sea, strange close encounters with UFOs, and even visits by ancient astronauts, reports from the Zone have been censored—even though the Zone contains all the peculiar elements of these famous mysteries, and more!

Research scientists working to unravel the secrets of the Zone have until now shunned the limelight. The code of the Zone has indeed been "silence."

Harry de la Pena admits that the logic behind the secrecy has been simple: "Our biggest single fear has been ridicule and the backlash of bizarre publicity," says the scientist.

Now for the first time, years after de la Pena made his first discoveries, the shroud of secrecy is being lifted on this intriguing and baffling place.

In this book we'll examine its curious phenomena and attempt to draw some logical conclusions. But beware, the Zone raises more questions than there are answers!

The Zone

The first big surprise about the Zone is that it sits roughly between Brownsville, Texas, and the Baja California peninsula.

It's actually on the doorstep of the southern United States—in northern Mexico. It is unidentifiable on the map, except for being near the point where the states of Chihuahua, Coahuila, and Durango come together.

The Zone has been described as an inland Bermuda Triangle; a Devil's Sea without an ocean.

But is this so surprising? Not when you consider this remarkable coincidence: The Zone sits squarely on the 27th (or Mystery) parallel—the exact same geographical latitude as the infamous Triangle and other strange mysteries throughout the world!

The Zone is situated in some fifteen hundred square miles of parched desert land. But gaining access to this inhospitable place isn't a formidable task. It's not set in some ancient inaccessible valley; no foreboding mountain peaks have to be scaled to reach it; there are no raging torrents or treacherous currents to block the way. In fact . . . you can just walk straight into the Zone of Silence. Whether you come out is a different matter.

And what you witness in the Zone may not be to your liking!

During the scorching summers the area is a barren moonscape, an alien world where cactus plants grow red instead of green, and snakes have albino-white skins and red eyes.

The giant land tortoises of the Zone develop pyramid-shaped shells and have piercing yellow eyes like none other on the planet, giant scorpions scuttle around your feet, and awesome centipedes grow to a foot or more in length.

Dirt tracks lead into the Zone but no paved highways. Some years back, when one of the local Mexican transportation companies decided to extend its services, it discovered that it would be necessary to penetrate part of the Zone. Drivers were always in constant radio communication with their bases. Once in the Zone, they began to report total loss of contact with the outside world. Radios which used to pick up the dispatchers, or the jingle-jangle of Mexican music from local stations, simply died. Or they might suddenly begin to play curious garbled sounds, described as being like music played backward on a tape recorder.

If these frightening phenomena were not enough, the drivers observed that needles on compasses mounted in their vehicles would spin wildly. Electromagnetic disturbances could also strike without warning, resulting in well-serviced automotive engines giving up the ghost and dying for no apparent reason.

It's easy to see why the navigators were soon persuaded that this was no area for any sane holder of a service license to drive. They flatly refused to venture their vehicles through the Zone, and plans for the new route were quickly abandoned.

There are human inhabitants in the Zone—but they are confined to an intrepid group of scientists holed up in a top-secret laboratory. This research facility, devoted totally to the study of the area's extraordinary wildlife and paranormal phenomena, is run by the state of Durango. Special passes are needed to visit the establishment.

The degree of its scientific importance is best illustrated by the fact that it was opened in 1978 without public acclaim or fanfare in a small, little-reported ceremony by no one less than Jose Lopez Portillo, then president of the Republic of Mexico. People who work within its walls are specially chosen from top research communities throughout the world—including some known to be from Russia's elite natural sciences institutes.

Meteorites constantly rain down on the Zone. One of its most spectacular sights is the almost constant nightly bombardment of space matter. The desert floor of the Zone is littered with meteorites of all shapes and sizes. In some places millions of them carpet the ground. To the casual observer they can look like the aftermath of some gigantic explosion: broken and strangely shaped dollops of peculiar metallike rock.

Or is some of this cosmic matter the shattered remains of strange machines? Because of the unique geometric formations found among this debris, some researchers seriously ask if they might be pieces of ancient spacecraft that once visited Earth.

Whatever the imagination conjures up, the astonishing sight of all these extraterrestrial curiosities is unknown in amounts of this magnitude anywhere else on our planet. Why are these heavenly bodies drawn so conclusively to this one spot on Earth?

Professor de la Pena gives a surprisingly simple and eloquent explanation: "Look at the Zone as a cosmic window to the stars. The meteorites, which are comprised of mainly ores, are drawn by the Zone's strange forces like a giant magnet, just as you see iron filings attracted to a magnetic field in the laboratory."

If nightly meteorite showers aren't convincing enough, consider this as proof of the Zone's unusual powers of cosmic attraction: "Newsflash. Dateline Chihuahua, Mexico, February 8, 1969. One of the largest meteorites the world has ever seen crashed near Parral de Allende here today."

It became known as the Allende meteorite, the largest of its kind ever to have fallen on Earth. Its final resting place after traveling billions of miles across time and space was . . . the Zone of Silence!

The Allende phenomenon has become, quite literally, a meteoric landmark. When scientists began evaluating its content they had to start rewriting the textbooks about our understanding of the universe, its physical and chemical properties, and, ultimately, the beginnings of life itself.

Pilots flying over the Zone report that navigation equipment becomes confusing and goes haywire, dials and meters spinning wildly. Scientific research teams have discovered intense "magnetic holes" in the Zone. Radio signals have to be boosted to unheard-of energy levels just to penetrate into this bizarre area. Magnetometer readings have confirmed surges that are stronger than the pull of the North Pole!

On July 2, 1970, a U.S. Air Force Athena rocket, a high-altitude research vehicle, blasted off from Green River, Utah, bound on its supersonic journey for the White Sands Missile Proving Range in New Mexico. It never made it. Instead, it suddenly veered alarmingly off course and inexplicably headed straight for the heart of the Zone of Silence.

The resulting scandal, the recovery of the rocket, and the disclosure that it carried a radioactive payload have been kept top secret and under wraps—until now.

UFOs! Just about everyone wants to see one—and around the Zone just about everybody has. At the edge of the Zone is the tiny outpost of Ceballos, a town where the locals still talk about the day a giant UFO overshadowed the entire main street. UFOs have buzzed this area before, but this one was very different.

Eyewitness descriptions reveal that it made no sound whatsoever. It was rectangular and appeared metallic, and hovered some twenty to thirty feet off the ground. Dogs howled, children wept, and old men and women fled into their homes. The tough guys in town stood their ground transfixed, staring upward and silently praying.

Night riders, cowboys on the outskirts of Ceballos, sometimes herd cattle through the Zone. They know nothing about the technicalities of UFOs or flying saucers, but they do reluctantly talk about strange round and silvery flying machines by day, and brilliant lights which perform dances up and down the steep and deserted mesas at night. They often see them shooting straight up into the heavens.

These rough-hewn men are simple and uneducated, but

they are tough, and tremendously proud. For them, a sure sign of weakness would be to see things that don't exist; and even more so to actually talk about them. We'll learn more from them later.

Deep in the Zone there are strange raised earthen platforms. Almost perfectly rectangular, some measure over six miles in length across the arid desert floor. They are no mere quirks of nature, yet these platforms serve absolutely no useful purpose for man or beast. Who would want to build these curiosities in such a remote wilderness area? More to the point, why?

We'll examine theories about the platforms, including controversial speculations that they are specialized airfields for UFO landings, even "gas stations" where power plants unknown to our technology are refueled from the magnetic forces of the Zone.

The Zone is rife with tales which boggle the imagination. Bizarre animals and plants, baffling magnetic anomalies, mysterious meteorites, wayward missiles, UFOs, and ancient astronauts. The Zone is only now opening the doors to its incredible secrets.

What's fact and what's fiction? We'll look into them all in an attempt to form some logical conclusions—or even deepen the mysteries!

Chapter 1

The Last Outpost

YOU'VE BEEN VERY near the Zone of Silence, almost in it, probably more than once! It was on the silver screen and you were in the air-conditioned comfort of a movie theater.

A portion of the Zone is in the state of Durango, where John Wayne and other cowboy cronies rode off into those famous celluloid sunsets. This is the area of Mexico which has always attracted filmmakers. It bears an uncanny resemblance to the way we like to imagine the "Wild West" was a century or so ago.

The breathtaking beauty of the red-and-orange-painted deserts and the steeply sided flat-topped mesas makes a natural cinematic backdrop. The giant lush green cactus plants and the rugged terrain are perfect areas for chasing bad guys and banditos. But the illusion doesn't end here, it only just begins.

Driving north from the town of Durango toward the Zone, you can still spy ghostly cowboys, floating specters shrouded by the choking dusts of time. Or are they real? As the mounts move lazily through the scorching 125-degree midday haze, you may catch an occasional glint of sun from a gunbelt or rifle barrel, and you realize you are truly back in time.

The men with tightly stretched tanned leather masks for faces have a color resembling mahogany. Their white mustaches are covered with the alkali powder of the desert. They pay little heed to outsiders.

Their lives are still devoted to herding cattle and riding the range. They've been doing it since their Spanish conquistador forefathers introduced the horse to the Western world.

Banderros Mountains

Two hours out of Torreon heading west and north, the colorful vegetation thins to the odd cactus, tumbleweeds picked up by the harsh desert wind, and gray lifeless scrub brush. Even the tiny one-cantina towns have now become things of the past.

The Banderros Mountains are on the road from Torreon to Ceballos. They loom out of the heat haze to become the most dominant factor on the desert floor. The mountains are black and lifeless, with twisting valleys and hills leading to the higher peaks which overlook the desert, giving an uninterrupted view from horizon to flat horizon in any direction.

Once these mountains were home to Pancho Villa and his tiny band of revolutionary outlaws who eventually toppled a government and took over the country. Pancho Villa's valiant defense against the entire forces of the Mexican army gave the mountains their present name. From the lofty outposts of the Banderros, Villa's bunch of desperadoes was able to control the area, springing lethal traps against the government forces when they tried to enter the narrow canyons. No matter how many soldiers were sent in to hunt down the revolutionaries, hundreds of them died in hails of bullets directed by unseen eyes hidden in the clefts of the foothills.

Villa's natural mountain fortress was as impenetrable as the nearby Zone of Silence is inhospitable. It remains today a monument to Villa's fortitude and the savage bloodbaths that took place when wave after wave of militia were pitted against their own Mexican brothers.

After the resilient Villa proved himself a master technician at desert and mountain warfare, he and his ragtag army swept out of the Banderros Mountains and the Mexican Revolution was to begin and end.

A few miles from the famous mountains is Ceballos, the last outpost of civilization before entering the Zone.

Ceballos: Last Outpost

Ceballos appears out of the searing heat, like a mirage. The small town is a Dodge City of the 1800s preserved. It somehow survived a 150-year time warp without any Hollywood types discovering its moviemaking potential. A one-street, two-store, one-sheriff town.

Not-quite-naked children play in the streets; their mothers peek out from a welcome cooler gloom behind half-closed doors of adobe mud homes which flake with tired earth-colored clay. It is still very primitive in Ceballos.

The males of the main street slump in chairs on dusty porches, wide-brimmed hats cocked downward in the direction of the fierce fireball in the sky. Flies buzz, children squeal, small pigs grovel in the dirt, and the men remain silent. Whatever secrets of the Zone hide behind their weathered faces, there's no sign that anything more exciting than a Friday-night cockfight ever goes on in this sleepy shantytown.

In the one-room, dirt-floored police department, gunbelts

hang on nails in the wall, liquor bottles, cards, and cash are on a large table; a poker game is in progress.

Police Chief Manuel Chaparro still wears his holster fighter style, low slung and slapping against his thigh. He stands up and greets outsiders with a huge grin. "Aah! You have come for the Zone, yes? Let me tell you, it is a very bad place. Maybe you need a drink first!" He laughs, pulls up a rickety chair from a corner, and hands out a no-brand-name bottle containing pale yellow liquid.

Tales from the Zone are retold in hushed silence with an accompanying aura of spirituality in Ceballos. Few people joke about the twilight world which happens to be their neighbor, like it or not.

Chaparro is gregarious, but the four other faces around the table look suspicious. There's no tourist trade in Ceballos, no bus trips, gift shops, souvenirs or trinkets to sell. Not one of the impoverished peasants in this human backwater is making a single peso out of the Zone's notoriety. And, if you believe the local talk, that's the way they want it to stay.

They have an all-too-obvious disdain for "Zone Jockeys" —tourists and researchers who sometimes come to the area in search of magic and mysticism, or maybe even just the truth. Take the scientists out in the distant laboratory, for example; they're obviously stark raving mad. "Maybe they're only a little crazy . . . somebody must pay them, eh?" offers Chaparro.

The chief's also quick to point out that the scientists must be "very top people" because nobody gets to go near the laboratory without a special government pass and permission. "We don't know what they are studying there; they keep it very quiet."

But according to one of the members of the afternoon poker club, anyone who ventures into the Zone for the sole purpose of "just finding things" must have a "fried brain!"

. . . "You wanna pay tourist monies—come, you see my pigs!" chides another, flashing a three-toothed grin. "They only joke," says Chaparro with a laugh. "They are very proud of the reputation of la Zona de Silencio."

Miguel Diaz Rivera is the only man in the room wearing a uniform. His faded khaki oddball ensemble sports a badge of office, and Senor Rivera is introduced as a transit official. He is one of the intrepid drivers who frequently ventured into the Zone during its pioneer days as a potential coach route.

"But I do not go there anymore. Why? I'll tell you why—it is a very, very strange place," confesses Rivera. He's not afraid to admit that fear and apprehension keep him out of the Zone.

"Years ago, our bus drivers noticed that radios would not work in certain areas. This was very much a puzzle because there are no mountains to block signals, no valleys where signals might go over the top. You could go to higher ground where you would expect the signals to be strongest and there would be nothing there. Radio sets and two-way radios would be dead, completely lifeless. Yet you could drive a few hundred yards and they would suddenly burst back to life. We had no explanation for this.

"At times some transmissions were so garbled that it sounded like the broadcast was being played backward. Now, that is not usual. You agree?"

While the Zone may bake in daytime heat in excess of 120 degrees fahrenheit, and plunge to near freezing at night, flash flooding from sudden, violent, and unpredictable storms can turn the Zone's bone-dry creekbeds into raging torrents.

Warns Chaparro, "Do not get caught in the Zone during the rains. Horses, or four-wheel drives, are the only way to get out. If you get stuck in a spot where you cannot use your radio, we cannot get help to you. It is a vast place; you could be lost for days, or even weeks.'' Adds Rivera, ''. . . or maybe forever!''

Chaparro and his cronies in the run-down jailhouse are unable to explain why objects constantly fall from the sky, or the curiosities of the bizarre plantlife and wildlife of the Zone. They just accept it.

''There are so many strange things that happen out there,'' warns Chaparro. ''I myself have seen things fall from the sky . . . bright white lights that tumble down through the air. Some that shoot straight up into the night.

''The cactus and plants are not like from this world. I have seen them growing red in that area. People sometimes take them out and grow them elsewhere, but they begin to grow green in a few days. When they plant them back in the Zone they go red again in a few days. This happens with all kinds of plants—cactus, brush, and small trees. It is a mystery to us.''

The chief of police will not say he would never enter the Zone again. ''I do not go out there any more than necessary. There are no people to protect, so it is a place I would rather avoid. I cannot understand the things that happen in the Zone.''

Chaparro is understandably proud of the nonexistent crime rate in Ceballos. ''Of course we have no crime,'' says the chief, chuckling. ''We bring our children up right. Their mothers, they tell them they will send them to the Zone if they are bad!''

Visit any home in Ceballos, and mementos of forays into the Zone are everywhere. Meteorites, perplexingly shaped and metallic, looking like highly polished rejects from an ore-smelting foundry, are displayed with prominent respect along with statues, paintings, and other religious paraphernalia.

Zone Historian

Guillermo Saucedo Silva is the former president of the junta of the municipal government of Ceballos, the Mexican equivalent of a town mayor, and considers himself the hometown expert on the nearby curiosities. In one special box in his modest home he keeps some of the marine fossils, odd-shaped meteorites, and unidentified rocks he has found in the Zone.

"This is a stone relic of a fish from millions of years ago," he points out. "I found it right there in the Zone. We believe that eons ago this whole area was sea; we live here on a former seabed."

He examines a piece which resembles a chunk of flat, intricately worked iron girder. "Some people tell me this came from an ancient spaceship which crashed here. It looks like a rock but it feels like metal. Look closely."

Sure enough, the two-pound rectangular object appears to have been cast, or worked, by intelligent hands. Crisscross lines in reddish-colored stone form a checkerboard pattern on the mysterious object. The insides of the small squares are filled with hardened sandstone or silt.

"We feel this could be a completely rusted piece of metal catwalk, maybe from a UFO from many thousands of years ago. It might have crashed here when the Zone was an ocean. The metal turned to petrified rust and the squares filled with sand and it all welded together when the area dried into a desert."

Whatever it is, and wherever it came from—our world or some extraterrestrial source—it remains a puzzle. Hundreds, possibly thousands, more like it are scattered throughout the Zone.

Silva is a walking library on the Zone's peculiarities. He has studied it for over forty years—long before news of its strange anomalies leaked to the outside world.

Silva sighs and reaches into his memory. "I think it was September 1976—yes, I'm sure—when the giant UFO came. Some say it landed in the Zone, but we here in Ceballos also saw it firsthand. Many people in different locations around the town saw the strange airship. It was nothing like we had ever seen before because it was so big. It happened between nine and ten at night, and it was hovering right above the town.

"We could not hear anything, any motors, engines; it was totally silent. I wondered how something so grand and heavy could stay up in the air like that. It began to descend and then it moved slowly over the town. Everyone was terrified and ran to their homes.

"It was rectangular shaped, and long, very long, about two hundred meters I would say. The outside edge of the craft was surrounded by white, green, and blue lights, which glowed brightly in the dark. Then it moved slowly out toward the zone." Silva stopped, looked around for approval, and then insisted very quietly, "I do not exaggerate—I am speaking the truth."

Silva is convinced that the platforms of the Zone have some connection with the "invasion" of UFOs, or the strange night lights which are often reported by the cowboys who pass through town. The nightly rain of meteorites on the Zone further enhances the townsfolk's feelings that they are sitting next to some cosmic gateway to the stars.

"The platforms are made of earth; they are perfectly rectangular and about ten kilometers long on the longest side. We, the people of Ceballos, feel that the platforms are for some kind of flying vehicles. Why else would they be there? Around the edges of the platforms you find strange polished stones. Maybe these are meteorites, or possibly ordinary rocks which have been melted by some great heat."

A gentle, professorial man, Silva also surrounds himself with tortoises, lizards, and birds from the Zone. Picking up one of his pet tortoises, he says, "Look, you notice that on top of his crest, the shapes are deformed. The shell squares have taken on triangles instead of the normal square or hexagon form. He is from the Zone. Centipedes, they are the same, very curious. They grow over a foot long and have body designs made up of ring shapes. I have never seen centipedes like them anywhere else.

"There are red cactus plants in the Zone which change to green when you bring them out and replant them here in town. I have seen strange plants out there that should have round leaves, but instead they are triangles. It is all very unusual. There are many more strange things that happen in the Zone."

Outsiders Beware

Ceballos and its peasants might have found fame and fortune through their link with the Zone. It's a town where your material wealth is measured in the number of pigs you own. The suggestion of just one taco-and-soda stand on the main street, and the thought of its profits from hundreds of coachloads of tourists every year, doesn't interest the folk of Ceballos.

But Ceballos has been invaded by outsiders, at least twice in recent memory. And it was these incidents in 1969 and 1970 that further reinforced the locals' intense privacy and their yearning to keep the Zone a place of true silence.

The first rush came to Ceballos in February 1969 when the great Allende meteorite crashed to earth in the Zone. Scientists from across the globe flocked to Ceballos and surrounding villages to witness the remains of this once-in-a-lifetime miracle from the heavens.

Having meteorites falling around their heads on a daily basis doesn't seem to worry these knuckle-hard Mexicans, but when a powerful nation to the north unleashes a sophisticated rocket which lands in your backyard, then that's something to get upset about.

That's exactly what happened on July 2, 1970, when an Athena missile, launched at Green River, Utah, and bound for the nearby White Sands testing area in New Mexico, suddenly careened off course and was mysteriously guided by unseen forces to plunge to earth in the heart of the Zone.

Historian Silva recalls the disturbing event:

"Within a few days military-looking officials from the United States were swarming all over Ceballos and the Zone. They said a nose cone had come off one of their rockets and they had to find it. They hired a lot of local people to hunt for the missile—and they gave a big warning: 'Don't touch it!'

"If we found it and got too close to it we were to tell their technicians immediately. It was something to do with radioactivity. We searched for a month, sometimes shoulder to shoulder in long lines, but without luck."

Locals recall the area being inundated with U.S. servicemen and civilians. And when the search parties failed, an extraordinary plane had to be called in to sweep the Zone.

The nose cone was eventually discovered embedded in a crater at the top of a small mesa.

"They made a wall of strange opaque cloth around the site. I don't know whether this was for protection, or so that people could not see what was happening inside. They guarded it night and day, and gave strict orders that nobody must come near. Then they brought in trailers," remembered the mayor.

"We saw men coming in and out of the trailers. They wore strange silver-colored suits, obviously, we thought,

.to protect them from the radiation. The suits had silver heads with clear faceplates, silver boots, and white gloves.

"When the Americans took the rocket away they also began to dig up the hillside, the entire mesa. They brought in hundreds, maybe thousands, of barrels and began loading the dirt into them. We weren't even allowed to see the nose cone.

"A landing strip had been built in the desert, and every day airplanes would come in and out taking barrels and things. They even took plants and animals away to study. One of my tortoises was studied in the U.S. They never told me why they wanted to look at him."

The town leader explained that the crash had made his people fearful that other, maybe more deadly, spaceships could be attracted to the Zone, but the American military officials had assured them that it was a freak accident and could not be repeated.

"So I asked them, how come all these meteorites keep dropping from the sky? You can stop them as well? They laughed at me."

Silva offers a unique insight into one of the fears of the locals. "Many people here are scared to go into the Zone. If they don't need to go, they keep away. Why make trouble with the unknown? I have heard about your Bermuda Triangle, how many ships and planes disappear into it, how many people have been lost.

"Imagine what might happen if thousands of people were to start wandering around the Zone. How many of them do you think might never come back?"

Chapter 2

Discovering the Zone

WHEN HARRY de la Pena pulled his tiny armada of pickup trucks into a gas station on the outskirts of Ceballos, neither he nor his academic colleagues realized the enormity of the adventure that was about to unfold.

It was a little after nine on a Saturday morning in late 1966 and the sun was beginning to climb toward its searing midday zenith.

On the dusty roadside next to the gas station a group of young children gathered excitedly around a boiling caldron. A few steps away a canvas lean-to was attached to the remains of a rusting high-sided truck. From under its shade a crusty mustachioed Mexican of indeterminate antiquity squinted in annoyance at the pesty youngsters.

The old man yelled at the raggedy kids to keep clear of the superheated pot which was being fired full blast by a burner linked to a portable tank of propane gas. They ignored both the old man and the heat.

Eventually they backed off when the peddler painfully motivated his aging joints, stood up slightly hunched, and

shuffled into the sunlight to stir the contents of his bub-
bling pot.

De la Pena walked by and ignored the roadside ritual of
cat and mouse which is played out every day on Mexican
highways wherever children find a "pig man" has set up
shop.

Inside the caldron was a whole young porker, head,
ears, hoofs, curly tail, and all. This is fast food—literally
on the hoof—Mexican outback style. Not quite as sanitary
as a McDonald's, but once the pig has been cooked in its
own fat it will be picked apart into tasty portions and sold
to passing travelers and local farmers returning from their
parched plots around the desert. The Mexicans value the
freshly cooked pigs; the crispy crackling skin is a special
delicacy, and saucer-sized chunks of it can be bartered for
a few pesos.

De le Pena was carrying a large ice chest and heading
across the dusty highway to a small store where he knew he
could purchase a good fifty pounds of frozen cubes.

There are three rules before entering the desert in a
vehicle: Always gas up before going in; stock up with as
much fresh water and ice as you can carry; and never leave
home without a wide-brimmed hat. These guidelines have
saved lives before.

Back at the pickups the scientist's companions were
marveling at the fact that since they'd passed Pancho
Villa's Banderros Mountains a good few miles back toward
Torreon, they'd occasionally managed to spot a cactus that
erred toward pink rather than the regular green.

An unaccustomed traveler through this area might have
dismissed the peculiar shift in shade as being the product
of disease, or thought that a cactus was simply dying and
turning brown. On close inspection all the cacti would
have been found to be thriving and healthy, but strange,
nevertheless.

The whole purpose of the expedition was indeed to photograph the cacti which are native to this area and known to grow in unnatural colors. De la Pena had promised cacti of not just shades of pink but red and vivid purples. The trip so far had shown a promising start.

As the party stood on the roadside the muscular, blond-haired scientist in his late thirties strode back with the full ice chest balancing on his shoulder. It was then loaded into the back of one of the two vehicles.

A handful of the children had left the pig man and were now hovering near the "outsiders" who had stopped to refuel in Ceballos. With cheeky grins, two of the older ones brazenly came forward with their hands outstretched begging for a few pesos in change. Much of the local economy for the dirt-poor families in these remote areas depends on the children begging for money from the turistos as they pass through town.

De la Pena urged his colleagues not to hand over too much cash or they would immediately face being surrounded by the entire junior population of the town. Robbery is not a problem in this unadulterated part of Mexico. Property and possessions are mutually valued and often shared among a whole community. The banditos preying on unwary travelers only exist in fiction—but pilfering by the wide eyes and friendly smiles of undernourished children is entirely accepted.

Loaded to the gills, the pickups trundled some 150 yards farther toward the center of Ceballos and made a sharp right turn onto a dusty track that headed into the desert and toward some distant mountains. Heads began hitting low ceilings of the cabs as they navigated across deep ruts in the primitive roadway.

Explaining that the rock-strewn surface was about the best they would experience until they came back to civilization, de la Pena was effectively assuring his companions that any discomfort they might feel now would clearly be surpassed as the miles of hardship wore deeper into the desert.

A Zone Unknown

At this time, two decades ago, the name Zone of Silence didn't exist, and it wouldn't until a few months later when de la Pena reported some of his curious findings to a young up-and-coming reporter at *El Siglo de Torreon*, the leading newspaper back in his hometown.

That journalist, now editor and general manager of *El Siglo*, was Miguel Angel Ruelas. The early meetings with de la Pena are still vivid in his memory as he recalls the scientist being "reluctant" to fully reveal the extent of the anomalies he'd discovered in the desert beyond Ceballos.

"Let's say Professor de la Pena was a little shy about telling his story," remembers Ruelas, now forty-four years old and a devoted student and active researcher of Zone matters.

In his plush office at *El Siglo*, the dark-haired, youthful-looking newspaper boss went on: "It was too fantastic a story for many people to believe. And I know that Harry feared being ridiculed by his scientific peers. I have to admit it sounded too bizarre to be true, but after many hours of gaining Harry's confidence I was able to piece most of it together."

To the staid, conservative editors of the Torreon daily paper, the existence of strange unexplained phenomena in an uninhabited section of desert wasn't exactly titillating.

Ruelas was one of the first to suggest that maybe it was an inland cousin of the Bermuda Triangle, an area a few hundred miles to the east of this part of northern Mexico which was then gaining peculiar notoriety in the popular press and even in books. The so-called Triangle of Death was even on exactly the same parallel of latitude as the strange desert to the north of Ceballos.

But, as later when he took a couple of years' break from journalism to become a lawyer, Ruelas's persistence paid off. He made trips to the area with de la Pena and other scientists and was able to witness firsthand the incredible cacti and bizarre wildlife. And he was able to experience the absolute solitude of attempting to tune in a radio in a place where radio waves will not penetrate.

"The simple fact that something was so powerful that it could completely obliterate all forms of radio communication was a powerful stimulus to a young reporter," admits Ruelas.

Eventually the editors of *El Siglo* bent to Ruelas's powers of persuasion and his abilities as an investigative reporter, and for the first time the strange area was christened with the headline *Zone of Silence* over the reporter's offbeat feature.

Ruelas was later to gain national and international attention by being the first journalist to break the news of the Allende meteorite in 1969 when it plummeted to earth exactly in the heart of the Zone of Silence.

A Mysterious Visitor

Ruelas was also the reporter who broke the story of a mysterious trip made to the Zone of Silence in May of the following year by one of America's premier scientists, the father of the rocket and the guided missile, Wernher von Braun.

It is still uncertain to this day what significance, or lack of it, should be attached to von Braun's suddenly turning up in the Zone of Silence. The tale certainly fits right in with the strange reputation of the Zone. But it was to take on an even more sinister aspect when yet another inexplicable event happened in the Zone a short while afterward.

Although the Mexican State Department was loath to admit to the presence of the famous U.S. scientist in and around Ceballos, Ruelas found through calls to the American embassy in Mexico City that the Americans were much more open and relaxed about the world's most noted rocket engineer visiting the Zone.

Ruelas was informed by the more enthusiastic American officials that Dr. von Braun's less-than-publicized visit was of no more significance than any other scientist with an exacting interest in space matters wanting to visit the precise spot where the famed Allende meteorite had landed a few months before.

Von Braun arrived by private plane, a Piper Cub, from San Diego. He landed on a small desert airstrip, normally used by crop dusters, near Ceballos.

For the next twenty-four hours or so, he was to examine various areas within the Zone. It has never been discovered exactly who his escorts were during the expedition, or indeed whether he had any guides at all.

But to make a trip into the Zone without native help or expert guidance is considered to be the ultimate in foolishness. The ancient Indian tracks and pathways that crisscross the desert floor could be considered as confusing and disorienting as the Great Maze at Hampden Court.

Yet von Braun was definitely there, and *El Siglo* reported the fact in one of its May 1970 issues, together with a stock photo of the famous rocket engineer. The article also stated that this was not von Braun's first trip to the Zone, but the newspaper did not elaborate.

Despite further quizzing by Ruelas, no American officials would be drawn to comment about the magnetic anomalies of the Zone, or its by then well-recorded abilities to attract heavenly bodies.

Such a worldwide scientific celebrity traveling to a little-known dusty spot on the map of Mexico was not soon forgotten by the locals, even though news of the visit didn't appear in papers outside the province.

Ruelas was later to shake his head in bewilderment when less than two months after von Braun's visit an American Athena rocket caused an international flap by unexplainably veering off course and heading, yes, directly for the Zone of Silence.

Since Ruelas coined the name Zone of Silence it has stuck, and even though the occupants of the pickup trucks on that Saturday in 1966 were unaware of it, as they penetrated farther into the uncharted desert they were getting deeper into the Zone of Silence.

Blackouts

The intrepid photographers of the 1966 expedition had been careful enough to include CBs and handheld two-way radios on their field trip into the Zone.

In fact de la Pena had insisted on it, as they would probably be splitting up into smaller groups and fanning out across the desert in search of the elusive cacti. Maintaining good lines of communication across such dangerous and foreboding terrain was, he felt, essential to good safety procedures.

One of the objects of the trip was to collect samples of the red cacti to see if, as legend had it, they would quickly turn back to green when transplanted outside the area. But nobody knew for certain exactly how many of the strange cacti they would find. De la Pena had assured them there would be an abundance, according to his previous research among the natives of the Zone area.

As the convoy rumbled farther into the Zone the photography buffs grew more delighted. No longer was it an odd, occasional off-pink cactus, but more of the plants were taking on the unnatural hue.

Just before noon the pickups pulled to a halt for refreshments and for the party to begin to coordinate its objectives.

Under the blazing sun the temperature was now well over a hundred degrees Fahrenheit and climbing fast. The wide-brimmed hats de la Pena had suggested were now a Godsend against the fireball beating down almost directly above their heads.

Anybody unfamiliar with the intensity of uninterrupted ultraviolet rays, beaming down unfiltered by haze or smog that doesn't exist over the pristine desert, will appreciate that an almost instant suntan is the least of one's worries. Sunstroke can be deadly, and keeping the head and neck covered from direct sunlight is a medical essential if the desert is to be survived for more than a few hours without shade.

As the group gathered at the tailgate of one of the pickups, de la Pena began to enthrall his companions with tales of the bizarre which he'd heard about the area.

There was the one about Senor Rosendo Aguilera, a prominent rancher and owner of many hundreds of acres of land in and around Ceballos. People say Aguilera was attacked by a manlike monster while camping overnight in the Zone with some of his peons. He had to fight it off with his bare hands, and ended up, together with three or four of his cowboys, chasing the creature into the dark night before eventually losing it.

Some folktales insisted that Senor Aguilera was himself the monster, a madman who delighted in frightening people away from his lands, which stretch well into the desert.

Then there were the remarkably consistent reports about eerie night lights and UFOs which were said to buzz the desert landscape on a regular basis.

The locals in Ceballos often talked about the strange

night lights which hovered on or around San Ignacio Hill. Invisible during the day, they came out at night just like stars to dance up and down the high mesas, across the desert floor, and especially on the small mountain named after Saint Ignatius Loyola by early Spanish settlers.

Of course, these were just tall tales, and de la Pena made light of them.

But the scientist could not refute the fact that mutant forms of animal life may exist in the area, because he had seen with his own eyes the shell of a giant tortoise said to have come from the wondrous place they were in. Instead of the usual hexagonal segments, it had pyramidal or triangular shapes. Although not hopeful, de la Pena secretly wanted to corner one of these strange critters for the camera.

Before packing up to move on, the members of the expedition decided to test out a set of walkie-talkies. It was the first diappointment of the day. The two-way radios were absolutely dead. Apparently somebody had forgotten to replace the batteries. With no spares aboard, the two useless bits of radio equipment were tossed back into a holdall. Frustrating, but at least they had the CBs in the pickup cabs, although they hadn't used them yet.

They broke camp and moved on.

By now the frequency of pink cacti had increased, and not only were they looking redder, some were actually beginning to display a deep purple in coloration.

It was only a few hundred yards farther on that somebody noticed static noises coming from the holdall. Sure enough one of the instruments which had been left in the on position had perked up and sprung back to life. When the second walkie-talkie was switched on it also displayed renewed vigor.

Using hand signals, the convoy came to another stop and examined the wayward communications pieces. De la

Pena was now mentally reassured that he had put new batteries in the walkie-talkies after all, just as he knew he had done.

But to be on the safe side they ran a simple on-the-spot experiment to test the efficiency and range of the instruments. One of the party took a handset and walked off into the desert, counting off numbers as he went. Well within eyeshot and shouting distance from the "base station" the numerical messages suddenly faded out altogether and only static was heard.

"Can you hear me? Over," repeated the sender, who was now some fifty yards from the trucks. He got no reply. His handset was totally dead. Frustrated, they waved him to come back.

And then something rather remarkable happened. The sender took a few more steps away from the vehicles when suddenly the walkie-talkie came back to life once more. "Listen, can you hear me now, over?"

"Yes," came the reply. "Loud and clear!"

"Well, I'll be . . ." said the sender. "There's something strange going on here; maybe there's a faulty connection in this thing. Let's keep going, okay? Over."

"Fine with us; just keep walking and talking. Over."

"Starting where I left off, about eighty. Eighty-one, eighty-two, eighty-three . . . ninety-four, ninety-five . . ."

"Hold it. Stop right there; you're beginning to fade again."

"I hear you, just," reported the sender.

"Okay, why don't you change direction, start heading to your left."

"I read you. Picking up again. Ninety-five and heading left . . . one hundred . . . one hundred and twenty-three . . ."

"Okay, stop right there; you're fading again. Do you read? Over."

"Sure, but you're getting fainter as well. Over."

"Just keep walking in the same direction and talking."

The sender did as instructed, but again the communications blacked out.

A few hundred feet later, and he was back on the air again as plain as day.

". . . two hundred and seven, two hundred and eight, two hundred and nine . . ."

"We're reading you again, as clear as a bell."

After some more minutes of "walkabout" the sender was called to come back to the trucks.

De la Pena was growing excited. His engineer's training and his scientific background in nuclear physics told him that something like this should not be happening.

Walkie-talkies do transmit on different channels but also on a very broad band of radio spectra for each one. These types of radio waves don't travel through select corridors, certainly not as narrow as they were witnessing right now.

Communications shouldn't come and go like will-o'-the-wisps, de la Pena told himself, especially out there in the totally flat desert with not even a blade of grass to intefere with the direct line of sight, never mind transmissions. This type of experience could be expected in a city where buildings with metal frameworks could block or absorb a direct line of transmission. But it couldn't happen in the desert.

Perplexed by the anomaly, de la Pena carefully examined the sender unit and to his pleasant surprise could find absolutely nothing wrong with it. In fact, it was in perfect working order.

To see if the same unusual effect could be repeated, the same person was sent out to retrace his steps but taking with him this time the unit which had acted as the base station.

To everybody's astonishment, the dead zones came up again in exactly—at least as far as they could ascertain by visual reference—the same spots as before.

De la Pena was baffled and overjoyed. Ever the inquisitive scientific investigator, he wondered whether he might have stumbled on his own personal anomaly to add to the stories of the strange area.

Over and over again the experiment was repeated, with exactly the same results. Then they decided to try it with the CB radios in the trucks. One truck took off in any direction while the other acted as base station. As the moving vehicle crisscrossed the flat desert for a couple of miles, the reception faded in and out and at times blacked out altogether.

"This is wonderful," cried out de la Pena. "I've never seen anything like this in my life!"

Even though de la Pena had a gut feeling he'd stumbled onto yet another remarkable aspect of the area, he felt too much time was being taken up with the radio experiments and pressed everyone to move on to their real photographic goal.

But they made a decision to keep the two CBs activated full time from there on, and occasionally over the next miles one of the trucks would purposely veer off and separate, weaving across the desert in an attempt to find more communication dead zones.

It was becoming all too easy to take off in any direction and suddenly, without even fading, completely and totally lose communication—and with equal regularity the CBs would burst back to life again without warning.

De la Pena recalls feeling like a young kid again, this time playing a bizarre game of electronic hide-and-seek that seemed to defy logical explanation.

The scientific wheels in de la Pena's mind were spinning. He thought little about the red cacti and more about his knowledge of radio frequencies, wave bands, time and space distortions, radar, and radio-wave blocking . . . and none of what he had just witnessed made the slightest bit of sense.

It was a perplexing problem. Why, in the middle of a perfectly flat desert with no encumbrances in any direction as far as the naked eye could see, should radio waves suddenly hit "black holes" in which they disappear—only to reappear again a few meters later? Were the radio waves being blocked, or were they being sucked into some transmission void?

The scientist knew only one thing for certain. Whatever was causing the disturbances was localized. It was happening within this desert area, and he'd not experienced phenomena of this type anywhere else in the world. The distinct possibility of a new discovery tantalized him.

Then he made an astute mental note: "Next time I come here, I bring a regular radio." This would enable him to perform a highly significant test: Would the strange forces within the desert also block radio waves coming from the outside world? Would broadcasts from radio stations fail to penetrate here?

The answer to these intriguing questions would turn out to be yes, but de la Pena was not to be able to prove the voids also affected outside transmissions until a later trip to the place he would then be calling the Zone of Silence.

The Red Cacti

There was no doubt that de la Pena's companions were impressed. The scientist himself was a little awestruck.

Everything that they had been promised was here. Right in the middle of this lunar landscape were red and purple cacti as far as the eye could see.

However, the strangest thing from a botanical point of view, noted one of the expedition party, was that living alongside the unnatural cacti were perfectly ordinary-looking green cacti. Why should two otherwise identical cacti be different colors?

There was nothing to distinguish in shape, form, needles, size, or even growth rates between the cacti—except for the devilish color.

On the outskirts of the desert the just-discernible pinkish tinges on the cacti could have been perceived as a slight mutation, a variation that could possibly have been caused by unusual oxides or other chemical anomalies in the sandy soil. But here in the heart of the strange desert there was no doubt that the vivid purple cacti were a breed apart. When two cacti live side by side and one grows up green and its next-door neighbor purple, it's the remotest possibility that chemicals in the same shared earth will be drawn to paint one bizarrely and not the other.

De la Pena made copious notes and covered his discoveries on numerous roles of regular negative color film, plus Ektachrome slides to verify that there were no spurious color shifts that could be criticized as resulting from the film itself. He realized he might also have a problem when it came to explaining to the color-processing lab that they might not believe their eyes. Even an experienced lab technician might try to correct the finished prints to show all-green cacti.*

---

*This strange twist also happened to my color prints when they were developed and printed at a Kodak-licensed laboratory in Torreon. Obviously, the technicians, seeing purple cacti appearing on the prints, junked the first run through the processor, shifted the entire color scale to the green end of the spectrum, and ran the prints through again until they were satisfied with almost perfectly normal-looking cacti. When I first saw the prints my heart dropped. How could I explain this to my editor? "Look, you're going to find this hard to believe, but the green cacti you're looking at are actually deep purple in real life." Fortunately, when the negatives were placed in the hands of photographic experts in the U.S., they simply set their printer's color scales to normal parameters and the vivid purples reproduced naturally on the prints—together with the regular greens of the normal-looking cacti for comparison.

Another anomaly soon became apparent to the excited photo group: When the green and purple were sectioned, their internal structures each displayed an identical green.

The cacti are almost impossible to handle, even with gloves. Their "prickers," which can grow to four or five inches in length, are as hard and as sharp as oversize sewing needles. These protective lances, which radiate from the plants at all angles, can inflict vicious wounds. And as a second line of defense they have dozens of miniature needles, almost invisible to the naked eye, which splay out from the base of each of the large spines. Anybody tripping or falling on one of these lethal cacti could easily impale a major organ, or even the heart. They are that deadly.

De la Pena pulled a machete from a trunk and with swings of surgical precision neatly lopped off sections of both the purple and the green cacti. He smiled to himself as he gingerly handled the severed samples. There was no doubt about it: Whether the cactus was purple or green, the internal flesh was identical in both color and structure.

Whatever caused these bizarre mutations, it only went skin deep.

Samples of the purple cacti were to be taken back to Torreon where they would be replanted and observed to see if, as legend had it, they would indeed revert to a normal green color after leaving their strange habitat.

But there was to be another astonishing find before they left the forbidding desert—giant cactus trees which also grew in the vivid shade of deep purple.

When they first came across an area which contained these oddities, the group stood and stared in awe.

"It's hard to believe. The purple color of these trees is out of this world. If I wasn't seeing it with my very own eyes I'd think we were on an alien planet," de la Pena exclaimed to his companions.

The bushy cactus trees vary from knee height to six and seven feet tall, and they each display a deadly array of thousands of needles. But the imperative fact was that they grew purple like their smaller cousins.

By the time the party decided to turn for home, and the reassurance of civilization, they had accumulated one of the most peculiar photographic albums ever seen in botanical science.

And in de la Pena's mind, even more exciting was the unique discovery of the bizarre transmission anomalies—a finding that was later to prove to be the first factor to put the Zone of Silence well and truly on the map as one of the world's greatest unexplained mysteries.

And, as will be revealed in detail in a later chapter, bio-oddities don't end with the plantlife—they only just begin. A whole series of mutant animal wildlife offers new intangibles.

One fact that cannot be ignored is the Zone's undeniable connection with other unexplained oddities on our planet— its site on the 27th parallel of the globe.

Together with the Bermuda Triangle, the Zone is joined on the baffling Mystery Parallel by the Great Pyramids of Giza in Egypt, Japan's Devil's Sea, the site of the legendary Tibetan holy cities, and other famous mysteries.

We'll look at these and other global anomalies for some plausible clues to the strangeness of the Zone before we probe even deeper.

Chapter 3

The Mystery Parallel

WHY THE 27TH parallel should be any different from the other latitudes on the globe is what makes it such a tantalizing oddity.

Study a world atlas, find the 27th line of latitude in the Northern Hemisphere, and be astonished at how many famous mysteries straddle it.

The Mystery Parallel becomes even more obvious when one starts to assemble a list of places around the world which have been famous for such peculiarities as missing persons and objects and an abundance of paranormal phenomena.

Dr. Michael A. Persinger, a highly respected researcher at Laurentian University in Canada, obtained a comprehensive computer cataloging of unusual or unexplained disappearances of ships, planes, and people and the frequencies of these happenings.

These were categorized into three types: 1) areas of anomaly, 2) areas of specific anomalies, and 3) areas of intense anomalies.

From left to right on the world atlas, the first spot

appears out in the Pacific Ocean (rated a 2); next comes an area covering Florida and the Bahamian and Bermudan chains (rated a 3); this is followed by a region of northwest Africa (rated 1); then a spot to the north of India and Pakistan, roughly equivalent to the position of Tibet (rated a 2); and finally a position in the Sea of Japan (rated a 3).

What becomes very obvious is that you can trace a straight line (allowing for the curvature of the globe) through all of these areas—and, surprisingly, "anomalous phenomena" do not deviate to parts of the world which are either above or below this line.

Strange? Well, that's what good mysteries are all about.

Is it coincidence that the Zone of Silence, the Bermuda Triangle, the Great Pyramids, Tibet's holy cities, and Japan's Devil's Sea should all be on exactly the same latitude?

The Zone of Silence has been mapped by geophysical experts. Its exact coordinates are parallels 26 to 28 northern latitude, meridians 104 to 106 western longitude. In other words, it sits exactly astride the famed 27th (or Mystery) parallel!

Vanishing Civilizations: Could the Zone Once Have Been a Thriving Metropolis?

The puzzle of the Zone becomes even more intriguing when we look further back into ancient history.

The 27th parallel is just above the Tropic of Cancer, the northernmost latitude reached by the sun before it starts its annual migration back through the equator to the Tropic of Capricorn in the Southern Hemisphere. What powers might emanate from the areas surrounding this latitude are unknown. But the further we go back in time, the more fabled places we find have rested near its arc. They are the ancient vanished civilizations of Ur, Persepolis, and Mohenjo-Daro.

These lost cities all have one thing in common: Each was at one time a center of a thriving superior civilization. Something unique had sparked an explosion of knowledge and wisdom to create breathtaking metropolises of great authority and power. At the time they were each at their zeniths, there was none comparable on the entire globe.

These wonders of civilization, in different countries but on the same global latitudes, were the most advanced cultures of their time—but they all mysteriously and suddenly died out.

Archaeologists are now suggesting that beneath the desert of the Zone of Silence could lie the remains of an unknown civilization which flourished somewhere back in the mists of time.

Because of the Zone's enigmatic magnetism it's now widely speculated that under its surface may be a huge layer, or mountain, of metal—a mother lode of ores which could have remained untapped since prehistory. A vast cache of readily available metals, which predated the Iron and Bronze ages in the European and Eastern worlds, might have been a natural attraction for the prehistoric folk who roamed the wilderness of Mexico.

Were early people able to utilize these resources to build a great civilization like those on the same latitudes to the east? Did it suddenly and catastrophically die out, only to be covered by the shifting sands of time which obliterated all traces of former human life?

Vanishing ancient worlds are obviously not a new thing. And the striking similarity linking them to the Zone is that they were all based in arid, often inhospitable, desert lands—geophysical mirror images of the Zone of Silence.

Ur

Excavations of deeply buried primitive layers at the site of Ur, in Mesopotamia, show that it was a thriving city as far back as 4500 B.C.

Today it is desert and dust, but then it was one of the greatest cities of the Sumerian culture, with palaces, temples, royal tombs, and even two harbors on the now-extinct watercourse through which flowed the Euphrates and a tributary of the legendary river Tigris.

Yet four thousand years later, by 500 B.C., it was falling into decay and ruin, a home only to human and animal scavengers.

Persepolis

Persepolis was relatively short-lived. It was built around 520 B.C. by the descendants of the Aryan tribes which swept down from southern Russia into the great plateau of Iran to become known as Persians.

These were a bizarre people whose history tells of their being plagued by demons, leading them to destroy all insects and reptiles believed to be the physical representatives of evil spirits. They also had a strange way of dispatching their own: Folk over the age of seventy were either starved or strangled to death.

But out of this maniacal society living on a parched desert floor came the magnificence of Persepolis. The city's public hall, the Apadana Audience Hall, was one of the largest enclosures ever built. It had seventy-two sixty-foot columns and took thirty years to complete. But by 330 B.C., Persepolis was history.

Mohenjo-Daro

The great city of Mohenjo-Daro now sits in what is modern Pakistan. It was situated on the Sind desert, another incredibly inhospitable place for humans to live.

Why it was built here no one knows. The plain is made up of barren colorless earth and stunted trees, and it's alternately blasted by dust storms or bleached by the scorching sunlight. Yet here, as far back as five thousand years ago, a grand civilization existed with highways, homes, and streets crowned by a magnificent holy citadel. Mohenjo-Daro, which translates to "Mound of the Dead," was itself deceased after just eight hundred years.

These great cultures were born and lived under the influence of the 27th parallel. Why were these ancients gifted with such superior knowledge and ability, while in other parts of the world, well away from the Mystery Parallel, other humans were running around in bearskins and loincloths, and living in caves and mud huts?

We tend to think we know just about everything there is to know about ancient cities and civilizations, but every so often archaeologists uncover surprises in the unlikeliest and most inhospitable areas on our earth. The Zone of Silence is one of these areas which is now being investigated for its archaeological potential.

Only time and digging will tell if the Zone of Silence is harboring the remains of yet another lost civilization.

The anomalous areas of the 27th do not have staked-out boundaries, and it is this lack of tangible evidence of demarcation lines which makes spots like the Bermuda Triangle so susceptible to misinterpretation and question. It's difficult to put your finger on something you cannot see!

But the Zone of Silence is certainly no figment of the imagination. Neither is the Great Pyramid of Cheops.

The Great Pyramid

One of the existing wonders of the world, the Great Pyramid remains for all to see and marvel at, even today after so many centuries. It is an impossibly great building of solid limestone with granite interiors which would daunt the ingenuity of today's engineers and architects—and still it was constructed to tolerances of thousandths of an inch when tools and moving equipment were about as sophisticated as the newly invented wooden wheel.

Tibetan Holy Cities

The mystical wonders of the ancient city of Shambhala raise more questions. Ancient writings, and the recent histories of the holy cities of Tibet, their magic and their mystery, conjure up unexplained visions of the paranormal and metaphysical. Was Shambhala afforded supernatural powers? Were its high-priest lamas really gods? Could mere mortals transcend from earth to heaven through Shambhala? Later we'll look into some modern-day accounts from the Zone of Silence which parallel the mysteries of Tibet.

The Bermuda Triangle

The Triangle is an area roughly bounded by Bermuda, Florida to the west, and a point in the ocean to the east. The entire area is on the 27th parallel at around 40 degrees longitude. And it is approximately four hundred miles directly east of the Zone of Silence.

Unfortunately, investigating the Triangle is like having a murder without a weapon. It's difficult to perceive magnetic aberrations or interdimensional faults, time warps, "black holes," and UFOs, without hard physical evidence.

But this is exactly what makes the Triangle, and the mysterious 27th parallel, so intriguing. It heightens the mystery factor, say proponents like investigator and best-selling author Charles Berlitz.

Do these sinister areas spread across the globe help to throw any light on our understanding of their equally mysterious brother on the same parallel—the Zone of Silence?

Numerous thought-provoking oddities and remarkable similarities between the anomalies in a dusty portion of Mexico and other mystery spots flung far along the same latitude are well worth considering for clues to the powers of the Zone.

First we'll look in more detail at the enigmatic Bermuda Triangle and the possibility of the Zone being its inland twin.

Chapter 4

A Triangle of Terror

SPINNING COMPASSES, magnetic anomalies, radio blackouts, worlds that turn upside down, time warps, UFOs, mysterious unearthly lights, stars that rain from the sky . . .

They all happen in the Zone of Silence. And the Bermuda Triangle.

The Triangle is the Zone's nearest neighbor on the Mystery Parallel and, according to geophysical experts, may be an inland "twin." It's therefore a good place to start looking for clues and dissecting some of the strange happenings which may help us understand the anomalies of the Zone.

One of the most extensively researched cases of a disappearance within the Triangle, which also exhibits many of the curious phenomena experienced in the Zone, is the infamous Flight 19 mystery.

Flight 19

The best-known, and still least-explained, case involved the multiple disappearance of five Marine Air Force bombers which vanished into oblivion together with a search-and-rescue plane that was dispatched to find them.

51

The TBM Avenger torpedo bombers took off on a routine peacetime training mission from their Fort Lauderdale, Florida, base. This incident received little notoriety at the time and was dismissed—both by military officials and the press—as a tragedy, albeit unusual, that would eventually be explained. The reasons? Possibly human factors like pilot error and poor navigational judgment, or even mechanical failure. This, however, was of no consolation to the widows, children, and other relatives of the unfortunate missing airmen.

Its mystery was compounded even more by the simple fact that not one iota of wreckage, or a single vestige of the airmen, has ever been found.

Even light bombers have some items aboard which float, the most obvious being life jackets, seat cushions, personal clothing, maps, photographs, even pencils and pens. Torn metal fuselages can also bob along on the surface for a considerable time. Planes have engines which need fuel and oil—and both these fluids float very well in seawater and usually form the first obvious markers of a crash site.

Sadly, the human body will also surface and float for a considerable period, especially in warm tropical waters, until it becomes a meal for the sea's natural predators. Yet here we have a situation of not just one missing aircraft and human contents, but five.

For this to happen so perfectly, logic would have to dictate that all five well-functioning machines went down in approximately the same spot together, into deep water (the sea in these areas varies from extremely shallow, even one and two feet, to drop-offs on the ocean floor which plunge hundreds of feet), and that not one of the crew members attempted to escape the fate of a single sinking craft.

Had the cockpits been sealed shut (even though it was a hot Florida day, and fliers in slow-speed hot-engined bombers are more than used to piloting with the fresh breeze in their faces)? Why didn't at least one of them send out a distress signal marking their position?

There is also another important consideration to take into account, one that has only recently been raised by military pilots familiar with the Avenger bomber. It is also backed up by newly surfaced actual filmed footage of this type of aircraft being crashed into light seas.

Anyone who has done a belly flop from a diving board knows just how painfully "hard" a water landing is. The new evidence shows that surviving pilots and crewmen of Avengers hitting the sea, at even shallow angles of descent, have described the impact as equivalent to hitting a concrete wall.

All the Avenger crewmen were fully aware of the appropriate action to take in sea ditchings—even if never having previously experienced one firsthand. They certainly would have had adequate time to discuss this eventuality among themselves and make preparations, unlike a pilot shot out of the sky who must rely on quick thinking and natural reflexes. Despite this, the possibility still exists, as remote as it is, that every single airman was killed instantly on impact.

This doesn't explain, however, how a fully equipped Martin Mariner rescue plane, manned with a search-and-rescue aircrew trained to cope with landing in even the roughest seas, should also disappear in approximately the same spot, 225 miles northeast of the Fort Lauderdale base, minutes after being dispatched to find the ill-fated airmen. The Mariner was, after all, a flying boat with all the most up-to-date technological capacity for landing easily at sea. It also vanished without a trace.

Into Oblivion

Our interest in this incident is not so much preoccupied with how or why the aircrew did or didn't survive, but more with what caused their tragic disappearance. This is where the question of the magnetic aberrations which are so common to both the Zone and the Triangle becomes so very disturbing.

When dealing with the anomalies of Flight 19 we hear about sudden radio blackouts, compasses that spin wildly, fogs, voids, and worlds that don't seem in place. An obvious conclusion is that they ran into some unseen force, one that was also unrecognizable or didn't show up on their home-base radar.

Based on the best official military accounts of what transpired after the flight took off into clear warm skies over a picture-perfect ocean, we find that the experienced flight leader, Lieutenant Charles Taylor, contacted the Fort Lauderdale Naval Air Station toward the end of the mission to make an emergency report which described his loss of direction and indicated that his navigational instruments were malfunctioning.

Additional radio conversations monitored by the air station noted pilots in the other Avengers questioning their own instruments with phrases which included the information that the compass dials were "going crazy"—phrases which are all too well known in the Zone of Silence.

Some of Lieutenant Taylor's well-documented words to base are as follows:

LT. TAYLOR: Calling tower. This is an emergency. We seem to be off course. We cannot see land. Repeat . . . we cannot see land.

The tower replies by asking for the flight's position.

LT. TAYLOR: We are not sure. We cannot be sure where we are . . . we seem to be lost.

The tower than instructs Taylor to bear due west (assuming, possibly, that wherever they were on the ocean they would cross identifiable land at some point).

LT. TAYLOR: We don't know which way is west. Everything is wrong . . . it's strange. We can't be sure of any direction . . . even the ocean doesn't look as it should . . .

With a few final garbled words Lieutenant Taylor and his entire flight, to all intents and purposes, left the planet and were never heard from or seen again. Like the radio phenomena experienced in the Zone, all communication was suddenly and inexplicably lost.

The Flight 19 incident typifies many of the bizarre disappearances in the Triangle because of the apparent connection between vanishing crafts and people, and magnetic disturbances which not only play havoc with compasses and directional equipment, but also leave the victims with an unexplained feeling of being in a void, a dimension in which nothing feels or looks right. Because it involved crafts which were not in the sea but in free airspace, it directly mirrors the magnetic anomalies so similar in the Zone, only a few hundred miles to the west.

Magnetic Aberrations

A catalog of the most commonly reported magnetic curiosities follows a recurring theme: malfunctioning gyros, spinning compass needles, total instrument malfunctions (electrical disturbances), electric power drain, motors and engines that suddenly die, complete radio blackout, unintelligible radio interference, and loss of radar and sonar.

As yet, not even the most famed of scientists in the electromagnetic and geophysical fields have been able to supply answers to explain these anomalies—although, as you will see later in our research, a very plausible one can be suggested for the Zone which may also cover the Triangle.

Deep in the Zone of Silence, not only is it common to experience complete radio blackouts, but the bizarre shifts in magnetism attributed to the Bermuda Triangle are also rife.

The big difference is that for the first time scientists can observe tangible evidence of these anomalies in the Zone without having to rely on first and secondhand accounts, often from persons who may have suffered some form of hysteria during their experience and because of this fact could be prone to exaggeration. This has to be weighed very seriously in the mind of the scientific researcher when applying a plausibility value to the retelling of an anomalous encounter.

In certain areas of the Zone, magnetic north is only a memory. Compasses can spin wildly and take on directional readings which are on a tangent to true magnetic north. Seemingly ordinary rock formations in the Zone will attract or repel a compass needle away from magnetic north.

It is easy to accept from these facts that the Zone can be an impossible place to navigate through when relying on compass or gyro. When faced with a bewildering array of magnetic readings and spinning compass needles, the intrepid who venture into the Zone can quickly become bewildered, disoriented, and hopelessly lost. Fear can set in rather easily.

The panic reported by amateur fliers, boaters, and sailors, as well as professional air and shipping crews, in the Bermuda Triangle is a very human reaction when coming face to face with the unknown and unexplainable. But it is also highly subjective without accurate, repeatable proof of cause.

But in the Zone of Silence scientists can now observe these magnetic and radiation phenomena objectively. Unlike those of the Bermuda Triangle, the anomalies of the Zone are not transient or hidden by an ocean of water; they are there to be observed and scientifically measured, analyzed, and recorded.

It is interesting to note that as far back as the discovery days of Christopher Columbus, Spanish crews sailing into the waters of the Triangle, and near the Zone of Silence in the Gulf of Mexico, reported in their logs strange spaces of disturbed waters on otherwise mirror-surface seas, patches of "glowing" white waters, and sudden unpredictably violent tempests the like of which the world mariners had never experienced.

Today we might categorize these unexplainable conditions and localized instant storm eruptions as possibly the results of unusual and severe electromagnetic phenomena. The maritime institutions of England and the British navy even had special instructions for their captains, warning of the bizarre navigational problems and unpredictability of this area which they described as "vexed."

But it appears to make little difference whether these frightening aberrations happen to craft or personnel at land level, on the sea, or in the air. At the present time not one single theory adequately explains what these mysterious sources of power, radiation, or magnetism are, or where they emanate from.

Within these zones it is becoming increasingly obvious that just about everybody shares an equal roll of the dice when it comes to experiencing the paranormal.

Psychic Connections

Psychics appear to be strangely drawn to both the Zone and the Triangle. These people, who claim to have extra-sensory awareness and abilities, profess that their extraordinary powers are enriched when they enter areas of the paranormal. The "vibrations" become more intense, they often say, creating a heightened psychic awareness and clarity.

Obviously the mere fact that the Triangle has been blessed with more than its fair share of publicity could be regarded as more than just a coincidental inducement to any "hungry" devotee of the psychic persuasion.

Nevertheless, variations of magnetic fields have long been suspected as being an influence on psychic abilities, especially ones like telekinesis, the ability to move objects by mind power alone.

Even the late Joseph Banks Rhine, Duke University's revered "Father of Parapsychology," tinkered with the idea that magnetism may be one of the forces associated with psychic phenomena. In a long interview at his home in Durham, North Carolina, Rhine confirmed to this author that he felt electromagnetic fields posed a big question mark in his mind.

The eminent researcher, who brought legitimacy to the study of ESP and other psychic phenomena at a university scientific level, admitted shortly before his death, "If I had more time left I would certainly devote research projects to look into electromagnetism and how it affects the psychic condition."

Electric fields and magnetism are now considered to be such a potential prime influence on psychic behavior that at Stanford University, Drs. Hal Puthoff and Russell Targ, researchers of the highest caliber, frequently utilize a Faraday cage in their experiments with "sensitives." The Faraday cage is a large lead-lined box, or room, which shields the "target" psychic from outside electromagnetic waves which may influence performance.

The magnetism of the Zone of Silence is without doubt one of the strongest sources on the earth, and this concentration may spill over into the Bermuda Triangle.

Psychic Experiences in the Triangle

In 1977 this author took up the challenge of a Florida psychic who wanted to be flown over the Triangle in an attempt to see if its magnetic anomalies would affect the sensitive's abilities. It turned out to be an unforgettable experience.

Page Bryant is a very large woman whose psychic bent leans more toward finding missing objects and people than seriously investigating geophysical phenomena. She is also noted as a successful trance medium.

At the request of the *National Enquirer*, arrangements were made to charter a twin-engined aircraft and fly Bryant over the Triangle. This was no mean feat, as the lady psychic must have weighed in at some three hundred pounds plus, and the pilot of the small craft was dubious about his ability to balance the plane with all that weight in the small third seat behind him in the cockpit. Nevertheless, luck prevailed and we were headed out toward the Triangle from a small airport near Tampa Bay.

One gains a whole new perspective of the Triangle's waters from six or seven hundred feet up. Unlike the view from a commercial airliner at a great height, undersea features are very visible through the crystal-clear waters, and so are the seemingly ever-changing currents. As an example of the clarity, solitary sharks can easily be picked out as they hungrily meander in and out of the various reef formations.

Although during the entire trip we never did experience any spinning compasses, green fogs, or sojourns in the fourth dimension, one thing became very apparent—there are wickedly unsuspected anomalies in the seas.

The first to be spotted were two giant whirlpools almost side by side, one estimated by our pilot at some two to three miles across, and the other even bigger, maybe as much as seven miles in diameter. They each had a clearly defined vortex in the middle, and it was anyone's guess what the central pulling power may have been. Both vanished after two or three minutes, but this assumption may have been subjective, as our angle of observation had changed. Although Ken, the pilot, had experience flying over these waters, he considered them a puzzle still worth discussion for days afterward.

It was some twenty minutes later when we had our first experience of the mysterious so-called white waters. Off to the starboard side of the aircraft appeared to be a strangely luminous patch of sea, certainly unlike anything we had ever witnessed before. Even in the strong sunlight it glowed with an eerie phosphorescence.

It was easy to see why Captain Columbus and navigators of his ilk were much moved to record this unusual sight in their logs. In a sea that's constantly on the move, the spectacle of a huge chunk of totally stationary, bleached water was awesome. Currents seemed to give way and head around it. "What do you think, Ken?" the pilot was asked. "Darned if I know . . . ain't ever seen anything like it," he replied, shaking his head in disbelief. There seemed no logical explanation for what might just have been a genuine natural phenomenon, an apparition, or just a trick of the light.

Later, as the plane banked to circle a large underwater reef, Bryant, whom I'd begun to think of as "the sleeping psychic" because of her noticeable lack of communication with the flight deck, let out one gut-wrenching groan! In a single horrifying instant the plane lurched to starboard as the full force of the psychic's weight thudded heavily against the right fuselage where she had been sitting. "Christ!" yelled Ken. "Get her upright!"

Bryant's features were contorted in the ugliness of pain, and perspiration was streaming down her face. Her hands were clutching a string of rosary beads in a viselike grip. Ken struggled to keep the aircraft level as I hung over the back of the copilot's seat attempting to right the slumped psychic.

She did not respond to verbal commands, prodding, or a couple of not-so-gentle taps on the face. The immediate assumption was that Bryant was in some form of psychic trance. She began to mumble in strange voices, one very high-pitched and feminine, one that sounded like a whimpering child, and at least two more which were deeper and definitely masculine. Some of the utterances (which were picked up on an already running tape recorder at her side) ran like this:

MASCULINE VOICE: No, it's impossible . . . we must stop . . . stop, I tell you . . . turn her into the wind. Oh, my God, no! . . . Come back, where are you? Come back!

CHILD'S VOICE: Mommy, I don't like it here . . . where's Daddy? . . . (*Later*) Why is he out there? . . . Can he see us? . . . Mommy, (*screaming*) I don't want to go . . .

FEMALE VOICE: It's not right . . . get us out of here . . . I can see a tunnel . . . can we get to the light? . . . We're drifting . . . we're drifting . . . Help us, God! . . . Lost! . . .

MASCULINE VOICE (*English accent*): Blast! . . . She's not responding . . . somebody tell me, are we in hell, or what?

MASCULINE VOICE: Is it a fog? (*Long pause*) I think we're being pulled . . . (*Alarm*) It's pulling us in!

MASCULINE VOICE: Hopeless! . . . Bail out? You can't bail out! . . . (*Laughing hysterically*) Does anybody know which way's down?

These recordings were taped over a period of twelve minutes, during which time Bryant writhed so violently wedged in the back of the craft that she had to be forcibly restrained in order to minimize the turbulent effects she was causing on the aircraft.

Whatever it was that she was in, the psychic snapped out of it to face an alarmed journalist and a very agitated and almost frantic pilot, who, without any reservation, was now heading hell-for-leather in the direction of the Florida coast and the safety of Tampa Bay.

Bryant was now clearly under severe physical duress and having trouble with her breathing. Gasping for breath, tears streaming down her face, for some minutes she was unable to speak. Her distressed condition prompted both the pilot and the writer to seriously question whether she was suffering a heart attack, or possibly some form of seizure, and consider putting down at the nearest available airport.

But as her breathing became shallower she began to recount, in between sobs, a graphic description of first a large airplane, possibly commercial, in distress (a garbled flight number was later checked but proved to be untraceable), and then a sailing ship caught up in some horrendous void which ended in its being swallowed by a fog, or the sea itself. She also alluded to being "on the other side" where she had met people wandering aimlessly and muttering. She had absolutely no recollection of actual voices or exact words, although she did admit remembering people sobbing, especially the plaintive cries of a child.

This author doesn't intend to voice an opinion on the genuineness of what went on in that small Cessna. Much of what has been described can easily be attributed to a very lively imagination and a certain adeptness in the theatrical arts. The full extent of what took place was never reported back to the *Enquirer* for fear of its being ridiculed (even this much-maligned publication has its limits), and a less hysterical, watered-down version was eventually deemed more appropriate.

As a sidebar, I consider the following (although it is highly subjective) to be somewhat to Ms. Bryant's credit: Even after a few days had passed she was reluctant to "relive" the flight or undergo hypnosis in an attempt to better understand what she had experienced. When the portions of the tape which contained the voices were replayed in her own living room, she visibly froze, stiffened, and looked genuinely terrified. After a few seconds her eyes widened and her head began to roll. Suddenly she gasped, asked for the tape to be turned off, and fled from the room in a flood of tears.

Golden Discovery

World-renowned psychic Olof Jonnson, a sensitive whose extraordinary powers led him to be picked by the National Aeronautics and Space Administration as the subject of deep-space ESP experiments with astronaut Edgar Mitchell, claims he knows some sort of ultimate psychic force is lodged in the "inner earth" of Mexico. He referred to it as "a zone."

Jonnson has also probed the Triangle. Knowing of the magnetic aberrations, he felt confident his powers would be enhanced if he worked within the Triangle.

As if to more than prove the point, the Chicago psychic spent only a few hours on a salvage boat owned by the famed treasure hunter Mel Fisher before he stunned the underwater detectives.

Together with a crew from Fisher's company Treasure Salvors Inc., in Key West, Jonnson, who was totally unfamiliar with nautical charts and had never worked with them before, unhaltingly guided their small craft to a spot among the Keys which, unknown to Jonnson, had previously been surveyed and "dived on," only to be "abandoned" for the time being.

The confident psychic stopped the boat and his heavy Scandinavian accent suggested, "You dive here, you find something. It is of much value. The vibrations are very, very strong!" The divers unenthusiastically pulled on their wet suits and air tanks and submerged into the clear blue waters, which were no more than a few feet deep at that point.

Jonnson had previously had a string of remarkable successes helping wealthy Midwestern prospecting consortiums pinpoint oil- and gas-bearing seams by directing his extrasensory powers over regular geographical maps, a technique commonly known in the extrasensory trade as psychometry. It was to be the first time that Jonnson had been tested over these waters.

As the divers were submerged Jonnson confessed, "There is great feeling in this area. It's a strong attraction, like a psychic magnet is pumping up the vibrations. I have no doubt that what I see in my mind is what they will find below. It is yellow and like a serpent."

Michael McDonough, a British reporter-investigator who had accompanied Jonnson on the expedition, was highly skeptical of the psychic's claims. "Olof was so nonchalant about the whole thing that I didn't think he was even taking it seriously," admitted McDonough later. "He had this ability to direct us so precisely to a point on the ocean, in an area in which he had supposedly never been to in his life, that I began to doubt his authenticity and suspect he was an experienced sailor with knowledge of nautical charts. I was later to discover that I was completely wrong. But I did know for certain that he wasn't aware that I had previously been told by Fisher's divers that the particular spot he'd chosen had been searched only a few weeks before—and was considered a bit of a washout. His mumbo jumbo about magnetic fields and cosmic vibrations didn't help to reinforce my enthusiasm about his abilities."

But sure enough, after some twenty minutes of underwater work, one of the divers surfaced and excitedly confirmed that they'd found something. What was it? "Gold, gold, and more gold," repeated the diver as he submerged once more. Before long they had attached a line to the haul and it was being winched aboard. What broke the surface left the onlookers aghast—and Jonnson smiling enigmatically.

Recalls McDonough: "At first it looked like a piece of old hawser or cable, probably discarded from a local fishing vessel. But as more of it became visible the sun began to glint off its surface. I remember thinking that surely this couldn't be something from a long-lost Spanish galleon; certainly not being found like this, just on the whims of a mere psychic! But as the crew members began to jump up and down on the deck, cheering wildly and hugging each other, it suddenly dawned on me that here I was looking at an object, possibly of considerable value, that was last seen maybe some two or three centuries before."

The relic turned out to be a phenomenally heavy twelve-foot-long chain of solid gold. It has now been added to the vast trove of treasures and artifacts discovered by Fisher and his divers, the same men who recently found the Spanish treasure ship *Atocha* in the same waters and can now claim to have raised some $400 million of sunken booty from the Triangle over the past twenty years.

Was this just a lucky coincidence, or did the Triangle's unseen forces help enhance the noted psychic's powers? Jonnson says, "I have no doubt that psychic abilities are increased within the area of the Bermuda Triangle. I have experienced it myself. I can only explain in words that it feels like you enter a state of heavy atmosphere. Yes, it could feel like being in electromagnetism."

An Eerie Prediction

Jonnson is also the same psychic with whom this author conducted a series of taped predictions in 1973. This was long before my own personal knowledge of the Zone of Silence.

On a recent review of those tapes, one prediction hit like a bolt of lightning. One particular tape was recorded over a meal in a restaurant, and in between the clatter of knives and forks and piped background music, Jonnson's very identifiable Scandinavian accent can be plainly heard:

It will be discovered soon, a UFO landing site . . . a zone [his exact terminology] . . . and will be to the south of the United States, I feel Mexico or South America. It is a very powerful area, very psychic . . . many people will dislike it . . . the words silence and fear will be connected . . . there are great holes in the ground, what you call sinkholes. I think they might be connected to voids in the ocean floor, holes under the Gulf of Mexico.

Although the Zone of Silence was never mentioned directly by name, or the Bermuda Triangle (which encompasses part of the Gulf of Mexico), the connections seem uncanny, according to our knowledge of the two areas today.

UFOs

Another strange phenomenon which pervades both the Zone and the Triangle is the mystery of UFOs. It is quite remarkable that these peculiar unrecognized aircraft are so common to both areas.

Is it again coincidence, or is there a definite link between sites of magnetic anomalies on our earth and the increase in reports of UFOs?

As well as viewing the "glowing waters" of the Bahamas, Columbus may well have been the first person to record the actual sighting of a UFO in the Triangle. It is reported that Columbus witnessed a fireball in the sky which first circled his flagship and then plunged directly into the ocean. In the language of the day he described it as a flying "bad," an aerial torch which trailed sparks behind it as it circled his small armada.

It's worth remembering that this was taking place during a time when the only things sailors were used to witnessing in the skies were stars at night and seabirds by day.

What consternation this unidentified flying object caused goes unrecorded. But in an era when the world was still considered square, superstitions were rife, and bad omens were viewed as warnings from God, it can be suggested that a near-mutinous crew might have been further convinced that their captain wasn't playing with a full deck when he recorded this sighting in his log.

Dr. J. Manson Valentine is one of the most respected researchers of Triangle phenomena and a former curator of the Natural History Museum in Miami, Florida. His interest in the connection between UFOs and the Triangle goes back over thirty years, and he has his own surprising theories.

During conversations with Dr. Valentine I was intrigued to hear that he theorized there could be some link between UFOs and the sinkholes which are evident in the ocean off the Florida Keys and the Bahamas. These giant abysses in the seabed are believed to emit fresh water, which leads to the assumption that they could be connected to inland areas or inland lakes; tunnels through which UFOs could travel undetected, using them as inner-earth superhighways or even subterranean bases.

One hundred million years ago the Zone of Silence was also a giant Cretaceous sea, known as the Mare Thetis—Sea of Thetis.* Today, along with the millions of meteorites found on the baked surface of this former seabed are curiously twisted forms composed mostly of metals. To many, these weird pieces look like broken parts of machines, even spacecraft, that might have crashed or possibly been abandoned in these waters many eons ago.

As farfetched as it may sound, this line of thinking also dovetails rather neatly with Olof Jonnson's prediction that UFOs will be discovered utilizing underworld passages that link the landmass of Mexico with the ocean to the east.

A controversial theory, no doubt, but one that sheds new light on why so many UFO sightings include reports that they plunge into the ocean, never to be seen again.

---

*Other spellings include Tethis. I prefer to go with Thetis—in Greek mythology, the sea goddess who marries Peleus and becomes the mother of Achilles.

During his studies of the Triangle, researcher Berlitz has amassed hundreds of intriguing cases, many of which I have discussed with him. A few directly involve UFO sightings, or exhibit UFO parameters without a "hard" object being in view. Some are better documented than others, but among them are these:

• In October 1969 a light guided missile destroyer the U.S. *Josephus Daniels*, DLG-27, was returning from Guantanamo and sailing north of Cuba when crew members observed what they could only describe as a huge moon rising on the horizon. The time was almost midnight on a clear night and the normal moon was distinct and visible in another part of the sky. One seaman described it as like a sunrise without the brilliance, or something that was a thousand times bigger than the moon. Over seventy crew members gazed in astonishment at the massive object estimated to be some fifteen miles away and which did not appear on their radar scopes, which had a range of three hundred miles. It was seen for some fifteen minutes, and because the bridge took evasive action a course change was recorded in the log. When the vessel docked in Norfolk, Virginia, admits one seaman, unknown officials boarded the ship, removed the log, and the crew was then instructed by the captain not to talk about their experience.

• A seaman on watch on a cargo vessel observes that his ship begins to turn in a tight circle as the navigational instruments go haywire. He claims a ball of fire rushes toward the ship and almost sweeps him off the deck.

• A small plane loses its instrumentation while being pursued by a cloudlike formation. Witnesses in the Cessna 172 claim they totally lost their bearings and the craft its position during the encounter.

• What appears to be a light plane is seen by hundreds of witnesses in daylight to plunge into shallow water off a well-populated beach resort. No trace of wreckage or survivors is ever found.

• On October 10, 1973, a U.S. Coast Guard cutter en route to Guantanamo, Cuba, had an eerie experience. Crew members reported sighting five UFOs flying in V formation over the ship. They were described as shaped like disks, moving fast, and changing colors around the red spectrum.

• Aboard the famed British cruise liner the *Queen Elizabeth 2* a crewman spots an object flying straight toward the ship. A hundred yards before it would have hit, the sea suddenly opens up and engulfs the craft without any splash, sound, or trace of wreckage.

• A commercial airliner is struck by a sudden terrific jolt as if being hit by an unseen craft in midair. The Eastern Airlines passenger jet makes an unscheduled stop to inspect for damage. Examination of the plane's exterior fuselage shows damage which is described as being possibly caused by a blast of intense heat or electricity. Crew and passengers report that their watches stopped at the exact time of the "hit."

The anomaly of a high rate of reports of UFOs in the Triangle and the Zone creates an understandable fear. But is it taken seriously?

One person who has genuine concern for this part of the hemisphere is the Honorable Eric Gairy, prime minister of Grenada. He even gave an address on the UFO problem to the thirtieth session of the General Assembly of the United Nations on October 7, 1975.

The colorful Dr. Gairy then followed it up by an unprecedented press conference in New York City. Sitting in an antechamber after the briefing in a Manhattan hotel, Dr. Gairy told me in a private interview, "No, this is not a tourism publicity stunt. We don't need this type of publicity. I am sticking my neck out not only in international political circles but in my own country as well."

In his impeccable English accent Dr. Gairy continued. "We are not only concerned about our own country and how undue fears can affect our tourism, but for the whole of humanity itself. Grenada is but a small and relatively poor country, but the specter of the UFO phenomena spreads much wider than our islands and seas, through the Gulf of Mexico, Mexico itself, and even into the United States.

"I feel that somebody has to take a world lead in getting to the bottom of the UFO legend. I fully realize that the United States had its Blue Book project to investigate the UFO phenomena, and I am very familiar with all of its findings and all of its faults, and this is why I am pleading to other nations to band together in a joint scientific venture to attempt to solve this mystery once and for all."

As of this writing there is no evidence that any other nations, apart from Mexico (interesting because it has its own secret government laboratory in the Zone of Silence), showed anything more than a passing interest in the prime minister's suggestions.

The official U.S. hard line, post–Blue Book—mainly from the military standpoint—has always been that until UFOs can be proven to be of any danger or actually harmful to our population, then they will be treated as no more than "interesting" phenomena.

An indication of the investigative malaise surrounding UFOs is the fact that one of this country's most popular publications, the *National Enquirer,* with a weekly readership of over twenty million, has for the past decade had an open offer to all comers (and that includes military personnel who have access to more evidence than the public might realize) of one million dollars for the first legitimate proof that UFOs are of extraterrestrial origin.

So far it remains unclaimed.

Chapter 5

Beacons from Ancient Times

A FORTY-FIVE-MINUTE DRIVE from Ceballos into the Zone of Silence, and a bizarre artifact begins to come into view.

It really doesn't look any different from other hills dotted across the barren landscape. A casual observer might dismiss it completely.

Gray scrub brush grows up the sides of the hill, which is strewn with boulders and rocks. Only when looking down from the top of this outcrop does an observer realize that the formation is surrounded in a perfect geometric circle by thousands of tons of rocks that shouldn't be there.

The hill is artificial!

We can also use the term "man-made" because it's safe to say the hill was not formed by natural geological evolution. Nobody can be certain that it was created by man, but common sense dictates that there has been no other form of superior intelligence in this desert region since it was transformed eons ago from its origins as an ancient sea—that is to say, if we discount extraterrestrial intelligence.

The hill is roughly a circular version of a pyramid in shape, although its apex has been destroyed by repeated attempts by peoples unknown to excavate into its heart, possibly believing it harbors archaeological or other treasures. It rises to a height of some one hundred feet and the sides are approximately at a forty-five-degree angle. Calculations of its weight run into millions of tons.

And the obvious question is, who would want to spend the time and effort to maneuver millions of tons of rocks across the fiery desert just to build a hill?

The Samurai Scientist

The anomalous hill was first discovered by Dr. Luis Maeda on one of his first expeditions to the Zone almost twenty years ago. Dr. Maeda is the epitome of a true Renaissance man: an investigative scientist, expert on wildlife, botanist, biologist, and fervent ecologist.

The brilliant man is not only an M.D., one of the leading cancer surgeons in Mexico, but above all he is a humanitarian who regularly performs his legendary skills with a scalpel without accepting any form of fee from the underprivileged population he devotes his time to as a general oncologist and chief of mammary surgery at the Torreon General Hospital.

It is fitting that many scientists actively involved in researching the anomalies of the Zone of Silence have long wanted to christen the hill after Dr. Maeda. But, so far, with typical modesty and reserve, Dr. Maeda has declined the offer, preferring that the hill be named after the "father" of the Zone, Harry de la Pena.

At the age of sixty, Dr. Maeda is himself something of an enigma as he bounds up the hillsides and mesas of the Zone of Silence with youthful zeal, or spends long hours under the scorching desert sun collecting meteorites and fossils, in pursuit of his passion to discover and learn more about this strange place.

On frequent expeditions into the Zone, Dr. Maeda's enduring energies under the extreme hardships of desert exploration have left younger and less experienced researchers awestruck, exhausted, and wilting in his shadow. This father of eight is an iron man despite his advancing years.

The surgeon good-naturedly accepts ribbings from his fellow Zone researchers when they refer to him as the "Samurai Scientist." Round-faced, Oriental-eyed, and with a powerful, stocky build, his looks reflect his ancestry. His father was Japanese and his mother Mexican, and, if his fervor to explore the Zone is anything to go by, he has retained all the legendary tenacity of his Japanese heritage.

In Torreon Dr. Maeda is a household name, a prominent personality and celebrity, founder of the Torreon Nursing School, founder of the Regional Museum of the Laguna District, and coordinator of the Institute for Scientific Research in Torreon. He is known mostly for his surgical skills and good works. His untiring dedication to unraveling the puzzles of the Zone is a little-known side of his enigmatic personality.

The list of dozens of scientific papers he has written on the Zone is impressive. They range from the exotic plants and wildlife to archaeological and fossil remains, and even from medical and blood analyses of native residents around the Zone to technical papers and reports on the infamous Athena rocket incident.

Dr. Maeda was first introduced to the Zone in late 1966 when with slight trepidation Harry de la Pena approached the eminent oncologist and scientist to discuss the very first radio anomalies he had discovered a few weeks before.

Instead of being laughed at as he expected, de la Pena found Dr. Maeda an enthused listener. The curiosity of the Samurai Scientist had been aroused, and from that point on he and de la Pena were to became an inseparable scientific double act when it came to all matters pertaining to the exploration of the Zone.

Who and Why?

One of Dr. Maeda's first questions when he discovered that the hill near Ceballos was not of natural origin was, who built it and for what reason?

It was a gut reaction that first led Dr. Maeda to take a closer look at the formation of the hillside.

He explains, "It just didn't look right, that's what drew me to it.

"The hill was surrounded by thousands of different rocks of all shapes and sizes, differing ages, and originating from completely separate geological formations. The combination of all these factors just didn't make sense. It appeared to me that for some unknown reason they had been transported to this spot from other parts of the desert."

Dr. Maeda's hunch proved to be correct. As he climbed the hill for the first time he found that it was mostly made up of a matrix of geological formations not native to the area when compared to the surrounding landscape.

Probing into the hillside at its apex, Dr. Maeda made another startling discovery. Under its covering of generations of windswept debris from the desert floor, the mix of different rocks appeared to be held together by some crude form of cement, possibly a mixture of the clays which today form the basis of every adobe building block in the majority of homes in this impoverished part of Mexico.

The land forming the Zone was once inhabited by long-extinct ancient tribes of seminomadic Indians. Their well-worn paths and tracks are still identifiable today across the desert floor—although, strangely, none lead directly to the mysterious hill.

"Right from the start it was a puzzle to me," admits Dr. Maeda. "There seemed no logical reason for the presence of a man-made hill, even in the Zone of Silence."

During a field trip with the author into the Zone in March of 1986, Dr. Maeda explained his thoughts on the strange hill.

"I cannot pinpoint any reason for its being here. It is a true anomaly. I have racked my brain for years to come up with a solution. Alas, I can find many intriguing questions and no positive answers."

Sitting on the apex of the hill, Dr. Maeda pointed to the circle of rocks surrounding the base of the formation.

"Look, ask yourself what are those rocks doing there. They must weigh hundreds, possibly thousands, of tons. Many of them individually weigh hundreds of pounds and more, and they've all been brought from far-flung areas in the desert. This in itself must have been a very time-consuming and arduous task.

"With that proposition in mind, then consider the enormous time and effort to build this entire hill. Although it would be only a small feat to build this hill with the modern technology of giant bulldozers and other mechanical aids, this would have been a gargantuan project in primitive human terms."

It doesn't take too much imagination to consider the hill as having originally been built as a pyramid, and the similarities with the ancient Great Pyramids of Egypt, also on the 27th parallel, make for intriguing conjecture.

The Great Pyramids have always been primarily known as burial mounds, but their alignments and structure also dictate a logic based on astronomical observation.

"I first considered it might be an ancient ceremonial burial mound, a relic from previous Indian cultures. But we have never been able to find one single human artifact, whether it be bones, tools, or other man-made utensils of everyday life,'' says Dr. Maeda.

The ardent conservationist and ecologist has to admit, ''Also, I am loath to destroy the hillside, just to excavate and prove this theory. Who knows what we would find in its center? Maybe we should not want to know.''

Dr. Maeda consulted with archaeologist friends who suggested it may have been built as a desert watchtower or beacon.

''But that didn't make sense either. The hill stands less than five miles away from the base of a small mountain range which clearly overshadows its potential as a vantage or lookout point.''

Was it in some way connected to ancient astronomical observation of the heavens?

An all-too-obvious fact is that the hill sits in direct line with a massive V-shaped cleft in the nearby mountain range. The positioning is reminiscent of the sights of a pistol or rifle, looking down the barrel through a V toward the sighting ridge at the end.

''Astronomical observatory was another possibility we considered. There may be some correlation between the way the sun rises and the shadows it may cast onto the hillside through the fault in the mountain range.

''There might be a significance in the way the hillside and the mountains behind it may act as a sighting reference to the stars of the night skies. These are possibilities that we are still investigating.''

Whatever secrets the hill holds, Dr. Maeda and other researchers are beginning to look to the Great Pyramids of Egypt to explore the possibility of supplying a key to unravel the mystery of this man-made hill in the Zone of Silence.

And they are seriously considering the possibilities of ''alternate intelligence'' being responsible for its formation.

Pyramid Power

Is a form of higher-than-human intelligence responsible for some of our world's great mysteries?

The Great Pyramid of Cheops is one of the most monumental wonders on the 27th parallel. We know why it was built and who built it, but the big questions is . . . how?

With the Zone's man-made hill (Dr. Maeda doesn't discount the strong possibility that there are other artificial hills in the Zone still to be discovered) and the existence of massive earthen platforms in the Zone, the questions posed ask not only how, but why and who.

Students of ancient astronomical research have suggested for centuries that the pyramids are heavenly markers, pointers used for alignment with the stars to aid in timekeeping and navigation. It has been suggested they might have been used in reverse—beacons which could easily be seen from high in the atmosphere, and used as guideposts for ancient flying craft.

But why would anyone want to build an entire hill and six-mile-long rectangles in the middle of a Mexican desert?

Investigators who have viewed the Zone's ancient platforms equate them to modern-day landing strips built specifically to withstand the enormous weight and stress of today's heavy superbombers. One famous UFO sighting on the edge of the Zone had residents of Ceballos describing the craft hovering over their tiny town as being as big as a football field!

Shades of ancient astronauts in both the Zone and on the Nile? But more about these later.

Pyramids have always been a source of intrigue. We even have a mystical truncated "one-eyed" pyramid on our dollar bills. Pyramids range from the sublime of the ancient Egyptian spiritual viewpoint, to the ridiculous of today's pyramid-power marketing. Some serious researchers have even claimed that pyramid shapes can exude energy—but mostly this theory has been left to the exploitation of hucksters who promise everything from sharper razor blades, super-growth plants, and reenergized batteries after just a few hours under their pyramids, to the farfetched notion that sitting under one, or wearing a pyramid on your head, will increase brainpower.

The Greatest Pyramid

On a rocky plateau near the banks of the Nile some four thousand five hundred years ago stood a young pharaoh king. Pyramids were not new to the area; they had been around for centuries, built by the royal construction companies run by his pharaoh forefathers. They were without doubt the most distinguished form of high-rise family crypts on earth.

What was to make the boy, Cheops, second king of the Fourth Dynasty, so famous was that he would outdo all the others, past and since. He would erect the largest personal mausoleum ever built; create one of the seven wonders of the ancient world; and unknowingly write himself into just about every record book that has ever been published since.

Like the earthen platforms of the Zone of Silence, the sheer awesome size of Cheop's Great Pyramid is staggering, even by today's building standards. Its base covers thirty-one acres: an area in which you could easily park the Vatican's St. Peter's, the great cathedrals of Florence and Milan, and London's St. Paul's and still have comfortable space for Westminster Abbey! Legend has it that Napoleon Bonaparte sat at the foot of the Great Pyramid and performed a few calculations which told him that the enormous mass of stone above him rising to its original height of almost 490 feet would, if dismantled, build a wall around France ten feet high and one foot thick. Its four sides at the base are almost identical in length and would originally have been 760 feet long.

The largest of the tombs actually contains an estimated 2,300,000 blocks of stone, each averaging two and a half tons in weight—with some weighing up to thirty tons! The king's burial chamber is situated in the heart of the pyramid some one hundred feet aboveground and slightly off center. To support the massive weight of the limestone above and around it, the chamber is lined with granite and its roof is made up of seven gargantuan granite slabs, spaced one above the other.

The outside of the monolith (much of which has been eroded, stolen, or otherwise reappropriated for less substantial local building works, a form of historic recycling) was faced with fine limestone from the quarries of Tura on the east bank of the Nile. But the lower courses, which are all that remain today, are a miracle of stonecutting. It boggles the mind that in an era when the only chisels available were made from crude copper, the master masons were able to carve the rock, and have it set into place by workers utilizing wooden levers, to tolerances of thousandths of an inch. The width between these blocks of stone, most of which hit the scales at about the same weight as an early-seventies Lincoln Continental (and some as much as a heavy-duty freight locomotive), measure one ten-thousandth of an inch.

Imagine being a stonemason and having your pharaoh pass the information down that he doesn't want to be able to squeeze even a human hair between the gaps in his pyramid. That's the kind of tolerances these craftsmen were up against. Of all the Great Pyramid's secrets, this is the real mystery.

Despite some other obvious mysteries of the pyramid, recent research shows that although the task of building it

was a mammoth one, it was not beyond the possible—
even when you have only palm-fiber ropes, wooden sledges,
and earthen ramps to work with.

What many previous historical mystery writers failed to
take into account was the natural seasonal rise and fall of
the river Nile. Although it may sound strange in a desert
land known to be as arid as Egypt, water could have been
one of the main driving forces behind the construction of
the Great Pyramid and its smaller clones.

Historians have now discovered that a causeway was
first built which ended in a massive ramp of rock and sand
which probably rose hundreds of feet in the air. This feat
alone occupied ten years of time. For the next twenty years
a labor force of around one hundred thousand men toiled to
construct the pyramid itself. It now becomes obvious that
not only was Cheops a great pharaoh, but he was also a
very astute administrator with a keen eye for keeping his
people at work all year round and therefore effectively
abolishing unemployment and keeping everybody happy.

It worked like this: A small band of skilled craftsmen
was kept on full salary throughout the construction. During
the fertile growing season most of the population was out
planting and harvesting, but then came the peak of the
inundation, a season when most of Egypt was under water;
this was the ''slack'' period for these ancient folk, who
were probably wishing they could collect unemployment.
Cheops turned this phenomenon to his favor, both politi-
cally and mechanically. It was brilliant public relations to
supply work for the masses during the inundation, and this
is exactly what he did, signing on ten of thousands of
seasonal workers. But it was a stroke of sheer genius to
make use of the seasonal flooding.

With the encroaching waters, more massive blocks of
stone could be ferried in on wooden and papyrus rafts—
and as the Nile rose they could be floated farther up the

causeway-ramp to the construction workers. No hauling tons of limestone on wooden rollers over miles of scorched desert sands; just simply float them in and up to the pyramid. The only problem left was maneuvering them into their exact positions—and how that was executed is still part of the mystery which makes it an ideal candidate for the 27th parallel.

There seems little doubt that as well as being extravagant homes for deceased kings, the pyramids were also intrinsically linked to the cosmos. The Great Pyramid is in perfect alignment with the cardinal directions of north, south, east, and west, and also the brightest star in the night sky, Sirius. It's on the movement of Sirius that the Egyptians are thought to have based their entire calendar and timekeeping.

Leading from the King's Chamber deep inside the pyramid are two so-called ventilation shafts, incredibly straight narrow passages which pierce through the core to exits high up on the outside of the structure. These shafts are believed to have been intended as pathways for the pharaoh's soul to obtain access to his body.

Looking up from the burial chamber through each of these shafts, you'll see the circumpolar stars in the north and the stars of Orion's belt in the south. This in itself is a remarkable feat of engineering when you consider that an error even as small as a degree in any direction through the thousands of tons of rock would have made this magnificent sighting impossible.

And other wonders can be tagged to the Great Pyramid. For example, researchers ask if it's merely coincidence that the area of the base of the pyramid divided by twice its height gives the ultimate mathematical ratio of pi—or 3.14159; that the meridian running through the pyramid divides the continents and oceans into exactly two equal halves; and that if the height of the pyramid of Cheops is multiplied by a thousand million we get the exact distance in miles between the earth and the sun!

The Meteorite Connection

Like the Zone, ancient Egypt was once strangely bombarded by meteorite showers. These falls from the heavens were also the rarest of all meteorites—those which bring iron from the sky. Unknown tons of extraterrestrial ores, it appears, have been deposited on the 27th parallel.

This fact was proven conclusively by the discovery of collections of ancient Egyptian ceremonial ornaments and treasures which could be accurately timed on the historical scale of things.

When these pieces were scientifically dated, an astonishing discovery was made. The fusion process needed to create the metals wasn't possible; it wasn't invented until thousands of years later!

How did the ancients of Egypt come by already formed metals, well before man had developed the ability to extract the chemical ores from rock and smelt them into iron? The simple answer was that they had acquired them from meteorite debris! Nickeliferous iron beads were found in predynastic graves at Gerzeh, Egypt, and fragments of iron found at Ur, in Mesopotamia, predate human knowledge of iron smelting.

Such celestial objects were believed to have been sent by the gods, and now many cult objects found in classical times in a number of cities of Egypt are being reclassified as being of possible meteoritic origin. A black stone built into the sanctuary of the Kaaba, in Mecca, has also been regarded as meteoritic.

Ancient Astronauts

It may come as no surprise now to discover that UFOs, another constant phenomenon in the Zone, were also buzzing the pyramids during the time of the great pharaohs.

Recent translations of hieroglyphic scripts from ancient Egypt reveal incredibly that Pharaoh Thutmose III first saw a UFO on one winter morning around 1482 B.C. As if to make the story even more fantastic, the records go on to state that the strange flying objects became more numerous in the skies over the pyramids—and eventually Thutmose was enticed on board one of the craft and even went for a flight into space!

Details from the hieroglyphic record describe the first UFO as a "circle of fire," and the inscription "it had no voice" indicates that the craft emitted no engine sounds as it hung in the sky. The writings then go on to say that as more days passed "these things became more numerous in the skies than ever." The new UFOs were obviously extremely bright, because they are described as "more than the brightness of the sun."

The vision of these small craft—calculated to be only some sixteen feet in diameter—must have been an awesome sight for the pharaoh, some fifteen centuries before the birth of Christ. Renowned UFO expert and author Brad Steiger interprets the writings as being a historically accurate description of a fleet of UFOs together with a mother ship when compared to present-day reports.

Biblical scholar Zecharia Sitchin, author of the book *The Stairway to Heaven*, takes the descriptions one step further. He believes the ancient scholars indicate in their writings that Thutmose "flew up to the sky" and observed the "mysterious ways in heaven." In simple terms, the pharaoh was transported by a UFO-style space shuttle to the mother ship, on station in orbit above the earth.

Sitchin suggests that it was in the space station that Thutmose was introduced to the advanced aliens whom he described as ''gods.'' After observing space and inspecting the mechanical wonders of his new surroundings, the Egyptian king was shuttled back to earth.

The whole story sounds pretty farfetched. But one has to ask, what would possess the ancient scribes to invent such a fairy tale? And how is it that their uncanny descriptions exactly mirror many of the important craft and flight parameters we look for today in serious scientific recordings of UFO sightings and actual encounters?

The similarities between the arid desert of the Zone of Silence and the deserts of Egypt are obvious enough. When we tie together other factors, such as the man-made colossi existing in both areas, the bizarre frequency of meteorite showers and UFO reports, whether ancient or modern, there appear some undeniable, possibly cosmic, connections.

Should we be surprised? Maybe not when it's considered that all these anomalies have another thing in common—they exist only on the 27th parallel!

Chapter 6

The Allende Meteorite—
a Key to Extraterrestrial
Intelligence?

WHEN THE ALLENDE fireball tore its way across the night sky of the Zone of Silence it turned night into day—and it was to turn some present scientific thinking upside down.

It is because of the Allende meteorite that science is having to reexamine some of its most cherished theories about the origins of the universe and the beginnings of life itself.

In fact, the most significant meteorite to hit the earth since the dawn of written history may offer the keys to proving the existence of extraterrestrial intelligence . . . life on other worlds.

Allende was to prove to be a messenger of untold value, a harbinger of new scientific vistas and unknown truths.

The great meteorite traveled across eons of lonely space to seek out its last resting place. Why it should unwaveringly have chosen the Zone of Silence may forever remain a mystery.

No hand, except perhaps for that of the Creator himself,

had touched this intergalactic relic since the dawn of the universe.

One thing is for certain: At precisely 1:05 A.M. on February 8, 1969, the great Allende meteorite hit in the heart of the Zone of Silence.

This meteoric event was to take place some three years after Professor Harry de la Pena made his initial discovery of the Zone. His first findings of radio and magnetic anomalies were to lead to the discovery of a vast array of curiosities in the Zone, including the presence of millions of meteorites.

Meteorite showers can be observed nightly in the Zone.

In a field experiment conducted recently in the Zone, eight scientific researchers stood together shoulder to shoulder in a circle and stared up and out at the night sky. Among them were de la Pena and the eminent Dr. Luis Maeda.

With a 360-degree view of the entire night sky, they were able to record that it was possible to see a meteorite hit the Zone once every two to three minutes. That is an astonishing rate of cosmic fallout.

For de la Pena, and others familiar with the strange attraction the Zone offers to cosmic debris, the Allende meteorite might have come as no surprise.

However, despite the millions of meteorites that rain down on the Zone during the natural course of events in this most bizarre of spots on the planet, Allende was without doubt to become the king.

Allende is a rare form of meteorite, a carbonaceous chondrite, containing metals, carbon, hydrocarbons . . . and even amino acids and water! Pretty much most of the stuff of life.

But what made the meteorite—the twenty-seventh (the number 27 crops up yet again) known carbonaceous chondrite—even more outstanding was the fact that it was the largest ever recorded falling to the earth—and its unbelievable yield quadrupled the world's known supply of carbonaceous chondrite matter overnight.

A Fire Sphere in the Night

Meteorites are nothing new to the residents who live around the Zone. But when Allende arrived they knew this was something very different.

Any person with just a smattering of knowledge about meteorites would have looked up at Allende with certain fascination. In Ceballos, where every one of the desert-hardened residents is an "expert" on meteorites, they stared at the sky in awe. And a deep fear slowly sank in.

This was no ordinary meteorite. It was totally unlike the regular nightly displays of cosmic pyrotechnics that they had grown used to.

In the coal darkness of the desert night sky the sheer brightness and size of the approaching furor struck stark terror into the normally unmoved folk of Ceballos. They could easily be forgiven for thinking that the sun was about to crash down upon them.

As the vision descended some believed it was indeed the end of the world. People knelt in the dust outside their primitive adobe homes and performed hurried acts of contrition, making peace with their Maker before he came to claim them. Others furtively crossed and recrossed themselves with the sign of the Lord.

From Chihuahua City, over a hundred miles from the Zone, the view of Allende was more tranquil. From that vantage point the vivid display of a white-blue fiery cosmic tail could be seen as a thing of immense beauty as it arched across the sky.

But for the residents of Pueblito de Allende the shatter-
ing event was over as soon as it began.

Of all the people to observe the crashing Allende meteorite they had the worst view. Because they were near the
epicenter of Allende's arrival and almost directly underneath it, all they were able to witness was an almighty
brilliant flash and an earth-shattering blast which sent shock
waves through their souls.

It would have indeed sounded like the end of the world
to these primitive desert people if they'd had more than an
instant to comprehend what was happening. But there was
nothing to herald the arrival of Allende for the folk of
Pueblito de Allende. The meteorite came literally out of
the blue. It could have been likened to standing directly
under a storm cloud when the lightning and thunder ex-
plode at almost exactly the same moment.

But when the dust cleared and frazzled minds tried to
rationalize, the people of Pueblito de Allende, whether
they liked it or not, had just been placed firmly on the
world map for all time.

The term Allende was to go into the history books.
Meteorites are usually named after the nearest recognizable
point on the earth to where they fall. The village of Pueblito
de Allende gained instant fame.

Aftermath

Next day in Pueblito de Allende, in Ceballos, and in
many small villages and towns around the area of the
Zone, special masses were immediately offered in thanks-
giving.

The end of the world had not come, and, despite its
potentially devastating impact, not one single person, animal, or home had been hit by the meteorite's debris.

El Heraldo editor Guillermo Asunsolo recalled: ''I saw

an enormous brilliant blue-white light move across the sky, leaving a luminous trail behind it. I felt sure it was a meteorite, but I'd never seen anything as . . . the only word is awesome! The experience was almost religious. As I stood there watching this thing I was extremely apprehensive yet elated. It imparted strange feelings.

"I remember thinking of the power of the atomic bomb and what destruction this thing might impart. Then it was frightening. Only some time before I had read a book, or seen a program, I can't remember which, about the catastrophic effects a meteor would have if it hit Earth. Horrific destruction, never-ending clouds of debris, a sunless world, constant freezing night, plagues, famine, death . . . these all ran through my mind.

"I thought I heard an explosion. I know I felt the ground tremble. Then I could hear all the telephones inside my building begin ringing. Calls were coming in from all the surrounding towns. Some people were very calm, others hysterical. Many thought the end of the world had come."

What if this meteorite had landed on Manhattan?

The cataclysmic destruction would have been incomprehensible. No skyscraper would have remained standing. The meteorite would have hit the solid bedrock underneath the world's most compact city and exploded like an atomic bomb.

The shock wave would have traveled through the dense rock with such intensity that not one building over a story in height would have survived; they would have been rocked to rubble.

This gigantic force would have spread through the geologic strata like an enormous deadly underground mushroom. Residents some sixty miles away in Danbury, Connecticut, would be hurtled out of their beds. Injuries would spread this far and farther.

In Vermont the vibrations would still be felt, enough to tilt people from ski-lift chairs. The Maine coast might be flooded by a giant tidal wave from the south.

And in Manhattan itself there would be total destruction and chaos. As well as the toppled buildings, shock waves would have shattered all water mains and electrical conduits in the earth. No communication with the outside world would be possible.

If the meteorite hit in rush hour, thousands of vehicles would be buried in watery tombs that used to be the Holland, Lincoln, and Battery tunnels. Bridges like the mighty Verrazano, the Whitestone, the Triborough, the Throgs Neck, the Queensboro, and the famed architectural masterpiece the Brooklyn Bridge would have collapsed, tumbling autos and their occupants to almost certain death.

If there were any survivors they would eventually be dashed against the underwater debris of tall buildings as the waters of the Hudson and the East rivers boiled and foamed in a frenzied tidal wave that would erupt and swamp the entirety of Manhattan Island.

There would be no escape from a holocaust that would devour millions.

In Mexico, civil emergency crews were alerted to expect the possibility of an enormous catastrophe. But as reports filtered through from outlying villages between the major cities of Chihuahua and Torreon, it soon became apparent that there were no casualties or even structural damage.

Scientists Scramble

As news of the great meteorite flashed around the world, astronomers and geophysicists swung into action to capitalize on the once-in-a-lifetime phenomenon.

Such a rare occurrence had the Smithsonian Astrophysical Observatory in Cambridge, Massachusetts, alerting the

U.S. Air Force. After a quick calculation of wind directions and velocities, a B-57 bomber to follow the winds was scrambled over the Gulf of Mexico and for the next seven hours it collected invaluable airborne dust particles which had been shed from the meteorite as it blasted through the lower atmosphere.

At the Center for Short-Lived Phenomena, in Cambridge, scientists rushed to pack their bags, like astroresearcher colleagues across the continent, and headed for the Zone of Silence.

As daylight ascended over the Zone, locals were already beginning to scour the desert floor and mesas for signs of the heavenly body which had so terrifyingly invaded their lives just a few hours before.

They were soon bewildered and disappointed. No monolith was anywhere to be found. Surprisingly, there was no giant crater, no scorched earth, no trail of debris or destruction.

As spectacular as Allende had been in the night, its impact on the area might have just been a dream.

But it was soon to be discovered that the meteorite had dumped several tons of cosmic wealth, and by scientific standards that alone was worth its weight in gold. For the researchers descending on the Zone it was to be an astrophysical birthday to top them all.

Weary teams of local police officers, who had spent the last few hours touring local villages to calm frazzled nerves and give assurances that the end of the world had indeed not arrived, were now to become the lucky recipients of Allende's last will and testament. First a few scattered fragments and then dozens of larger pieces of the meteorite were brought to the officers for safekeeping.

In Hacienda de Santa Anna, farmer Promuncio Garibay posed proudly for photographs with his two young sons as they displayed their football-sized chunk of Allende. They had found the grayish black oval rock some two hundred meters from their home—which, they pointed out with some relief, only has a thin tin roof.

The offices of the newspaper *El Correo de Parral* became the mortuary for the last remains of Allende. Editor Ruben Rocha Chavez meticulously weighed and logged in each new find with the care of a museum curator. They ranged in size from a few grams to almost twenty pounds.

As Chavez picked up one piece to examine it he cast his memory back to his scant knowledge of meteorites and space, and a thought came to mind. And suddenly he felt very humble. It was possible that nothing had touched this piece of rock since the dawn of creation.

Hordes of people came to stare in awe at the pieces.

"I don't know, they look like normal meteorites to me," admitted one spectator. "I expected something much, much bigger!"

Policeman Arturo Rodriguez, an officer from Hidalgo de Parral, became custodian of one of the largest individual finds. This sixteen-pound fragment of the meteorite was discovered embedded in a dirt road about a mile north of the tiny village of San Juan. Its shallow crater, only five inches deep and eight across, showed the meteorite had hit with little force of impact. This suggested another puzzle.

The Birth and Death of Allende

The Allende meteorite had itself become a mystery. It had crossed the farthest reaches of the universe—an incalculable distance in miles that would need more zeros than could fill this page—at speeds which we cannot even imagine.

And it had screamed unhaltingly toward the earth, its remaining tons to land directly in the Zone of Silence—almost without making a dent!

With all the energy potential to create a holocaust, this firestorm from space, in its last seconds, dropped to earth with little more than a whimper.

The actual velocity of incoming meteorites is staggering. These space wanderers rocket along through the universe at astronomical speeds, estimated to top ninety thousand miles per hour. At that rate you could make fifteen round trips between New York and Los Angeles in an hour.

When a meteorite heading toward Earth enters our atmosphere, it is blasting in at speeds between twenty-five thousand and forty-seven thousand miles per hour, or a top speed of about Mach 70 plus! The world's fastest commercial airliner, the British- and French-made Concorde, streaks along at a leisurely Mach 2.

But strange things happens to meteorites once they reach the point of no return and are captured within the earth's gravitational field. With the help of their fantastic speed and the laws of nature, they can begin to disintegrate.

Allende committed suicide not far above the earth. It self-destructed before it could inflict any of its potentially massive damage on the Zone.

From eyewitness accounts, scientists are now certain that somewhere over the Zone the fireball split into two with a gigantic explosion. This would have been the earth-shaking blast experienced by the people of Pueblito de Allende and felt as far away as Chihuahua City by newspaper editor Asunsolo.

In a matter of seconds the might of Allende was history. It broke into thousands of pieces and scattered harmlessly over many square kilometers of the Zone.

Because of the millions of smaller meteorites which are found only in the Zone, we can simply make wild guesses at how many of them may have been born of a meteorite even greater than Allende when they tumbled from the sky eons ago in the days of prehistory. Many earlier space giants may also have been strangely attracted to the Zone, but we have no scientific way of putting the pieces together. They will forever remain a mystery.

With Allende it was a different story. Every chunk that fractured away from the parent meteorite could be positively identified. And that is why the scientists were scurrying to the Zone of Silence posthaste.

As a meteorite plows toward Earth it absorbs radiations from space. Different meteorites might absorb these rays at different rates, so that when each one lands it has its own individual radioactive "fingerprint." Even the tiniest part of Allende would have the same fingerprint as the largest. By taking radioactive readings of each piece, the scientists can be absolutely positive that they came from the same mother meteorite. But this radioactivity is short-lived, and that's why we cannot analyze "old" meteorites in an attempt to piece them together like a jigsaw puzzle.

On the night of February 8, 1969, when humble folk knelt in prayer to witness the end of the world, this, in scientific terms, is what really happened.

When Allende entered the atmosphere its fantastic supersonic speed generated a series of supersonic shock waves, explosive sonic booms, over wherever it passed. It was quickly collecting a nose cap of ionized air. This began to grow and flashed into a brilliant luminescence.

At the same time the forward surface of the great meteorite became white hot, melting into tiny droplets which were swept off to form a huge trail of fantastic light.

Whistling, whining, and hissing noises were also heard, and these are believed to have been caused by ionized masses of air.

Some six to ten miles above the earth's surface Allende exploded violently enough to separate into two distinct masses. They were then to disintegrate even further, appearing like sparks flying off a giant Catherine wheel.

The meteorite now became extinct, lifeless and invisible, as its remnants hit the desert in a deluge as large as 150 square miles.

But continuing scientific analysis of Allende has now shown it to be far from dead. A fascinating giant among meteorites, it has become a crucial key to unlocking the mysteries of life itself, and even unraveling the possibility of intelligence in other parts of the universe.

Was Allende an Extraterrestrial Messenger?

Dr. E. L. Fireman, of the Smithsonian Astrophysical Observatory, made this prediction back in May of 1969: ". . . Allende will probably be the most extensively studied of all meteorites." He was absolutely correct.

Because our present capacity for manned space travel is for the moment limited to our own solar system, meteorites from beyond are our only clues to what's been going on for billions of years on the outside.

Allende's physical appearance is of a dark gray rocklike material. It contains chrondules, tiny spheres of almost pure glass. And it yielded familiar names like carbon, sulfur, calcium, iron, sodium, aluminum, potassium, chromium, cobalt, and a whole host of other elements with far more exotic names which are all common to our earth.

More surprises were in store.

Scientists at the University of Texas and the University of Chicago estimated the age of Allende to be 4.5 billion years. Its birthplace was placed in the carbon-rich zone of a star which was six to eight times the size of our own sun, possibly during a supernova explosion at the time the Solar System was formed.

Some researchers discovered that Allende contained a

totally unique form of aluminum—aluminum 26. What makes this so fascinating is that aluminum 26 is believed to be a short-lived species which was formed during the origin of the universe.

Another startling clue to its great age was uncovered in Allende's fascinating chrondules. Practically pure xenon 129 was found. This is a by-product of the long-extinct radioactivity of iodine 129, which was created when the elements were born. Confirms the Smithsonian's Dr. Fireman, "The chrondules of Allende must have originated very soon after the formation of the elements."

And Allende, it seems certain, was a virgin meteorite, one of the earliest objects formed. Incredibly, it remained untouched during its fantastic voyage across the universe to the Zone of Silence.

Scientists in the Department of Geology and Division of Metallurgy and Materials Science at Case Western Reserve University, Cleveland, Ohio, concluded after analyzing samples, "The Allende meteorite has experienced no significant thermal event since its origin. At the same time, the lack of deformation suggests that the meteorite has suffered no significant collisions in that time as well."

In the vastness of space with its trillions of stars and planets, supernovas, white dwarfs, black holes, and an infinity of cosmic debris, the odds against Allende not bumping into something during its light-years "on the road" seem phenomenal. Was its course to the Zone of Silence predestined by some much higher intelligence?

Allende contained many elements we find on Earth. Hidden deep in its molecular structure were all the ingredients we expect to see for the formation of life as we know it—including amino acids. Should we be shocked? Not really. As chemists and physicists learn more about our universe, the odds against our being alone shorten all the time.

When a scientific gift like Allende lands, it serves to magnificently reaffirm theories that at the time of the Big Bang countless other suns similar to our own were formed with their corresponding planets, which contained all the same star stuff as our own. Why some of them should have had the same combinations of chemicals and gases that our own earth had at its inception is hard not to imagine.

They may not have happened on the same time scale as Planet Earth. The same primordial soup that formed on our world could have formed millions of years later on other planets, or even millions of years previous to Earth. And under the latter conditions, that suggests that there could be life existing elsewhere that may be millions of years more advanced than our own.

Which brings us to two of the most astonishing discoveries about this space invader from the Zone of Silence. Allende's composition is close to that of Earth—closer than the very rocks which we now know to form our nearest neighbor, the moon!

What the scientists saw in Allende is what is believed to have occurred during the early stages of the evolution of the earth. An interstellar twin from millions of light-years away? A fantastic thought, but one that doesn't now seem too farfetched.

Physicists Dr. M. G. Seitz and Dr. I. Kushiro of the Geophysical Laboratory of the Carnegie Institute in Washington, D.C., found that the major chemicals in Allende were almost the same as those believed to be in the mantle material of our own planet. In a laboratory experiment the scientists found that a melt of the meteorite contained 47 percent iron, 25 percent nickel, and 24 percent sulfur—a mixture remarkably similar to the white-hot molten core of Earth. They concluded that Allende was "closer in major element abundances'' than the ''average composition of the moon.''

Amino acids are the building blocks of life. They form the proteins out of which every living thing is made. DNA, the command network which controls our very existence, how we were biologically formed and continue to re-form, is made up of a chain of acids.

Yet in a meteorite from somewhere in infinity we discover numerous amino acids, among them valine, alanine, glycine, proline, aspartic acid, and glutamic acid—all prominent in earthly animal and plant proteins.

Is this just an incredible coincidence? Was Allende once an embryonic Earth which failed to develop?

One theory holds that our own earth may have started out life as a meteorite which originated at a time when the ''dust'' of solar nebulae was falling together to form solid bodies. In effect they then became celestial vacuum cleaners, sweeping along through space attracting all the debris straying into their paths. Some, like our Earth, accumulated great mass and their interiors heated up. Solar gases, steam, and vaporized rock stuck to the outer skin like glue, and eventually Earth gave birth to its primordial atmosphere.

Some meteorites obviously weren't so lucky, never achieving any weight or size. They were destined to become space nomads traveling time for eternity. Maybe Allende was one of them.

Creating Life out of Cosmic Dust

Physicist Dr. Cyril Ponnamperuma has shown in his Maryland laboratory that it's possible to create a crucible of life, given the right elements and conditions.

His research into meteorites like Allende, and the amino acids they carry in their molecular ''holds,'' has caused scientists to stop and think again about the creation of life as we know it.

Dr. Ponnamperuma, a brilliant scientist who is director of the laboratory of Chemical Evolution at the University of Maryland in College Park, raises fascinating thoughts about the possibility of life elsewhere in the universe.

"When we examine meteorites and find amino acids in them together with the common elements we find on Earth, the only logical question is: Why hasn't life evolved elsewhere in the universe?" asks Ponnamperuma.

"If a meteorite has all the ingredients that we know existed in our own primordial soup to create life on Earth, it seems highly logical that given similar atmospheric conditions, light-years away in another galaxy, a similar form of life might evolve.

"We therefore have a situation which suggests that meteorites which crash into our earth carrying amino acids may be harboring the genetic ingredients of life-forms that could have originated light-years away. This does not mean to say that our Hollywood image of E.T. is practical, but neither does it say it is impossible."

What are the chances of E.T.-type beings existing elsewhere in the universe? "It is almost impossible to answer," admits Ponnamperuma. "A single-celled animal, or possibly as a highly advanced form of civilization, the number of combinations for different forms of life are almost incalculable. Just look around at the millions of different life-forms we have on Earth—and they have all been generated from the same handful of chemical elements.

"The amino acids we see contained in extraterrestrial meteorites appear to indicate that the primitive starts to life had already been activated—although this is still a long way from complete proteins and cells that can reproduce themselves. But there again we do not know how long the process has been going on from whichever corner of the universe these space rocks originated.''

There's no doubt that before Allende blasted into our atmosphere to hit the Zone of Silence, it contained the stuff of life. The chemicals embedded deep in its chrondules were not items it picked up coming through our environment.

It is difficult for us to imagine that the same chemicals contained in meteorites could actually spawn life. And, after all, it has taken millions of years for those same raw chemicals to develop on Earth to the stage of massive complexity which forms a human.

But in the laboratory, Dr. Ponnamperuma and his researchers have achieved the impossible—they have created the origins of life from cosmic materials!

Crucible of Life

A brown goo of a liquid bubbles in a large spherical glass container. Attached to it are slim glass tubelets through which perk gaseous materials. A strange assortment of electrodes and wires leads from the apparatus to output and input controls. The white-coated scientists peer in to wonder at what sort of miracle they are creating.

The glass chamber is a miniature Earth, and the strange brew contains all the elements which were available on its surface millions of years ago. The tubes are feeding in the gases that existed at this time: hydrogen, ammonia, methane, formaldehyde, and others. The crackling electrodes provide a likeness of prehistoric lightning and atmospheric electrical charges.

The result—an exact replica of the primordial soup which once existed on Earth. But would it generate life?

After hours of activation, Dr. Ponnamperuma held his breath in anticipation. Microscopic analysis was to confirm a mind-boggling breakthrough. He had created the incredible—a duplication of the origins of life, millions of years later in Maryland, U.S.A.!

"When we analyzed our soup we found the existence of simple proteins. Only basic chemical elements were present at the start of the experiment. What we feel we had created were the very basics of life," explained Ponnamperuma.

This amazing experiment has since been duplicted a number of times. It proves beyond doubt that given the right conditions, chemicals from Earth and those contained in meteorites can sprout the origins of life.

Allende, the intergalactic messenger to the Zone of Silence, tells us that the conditions for life elsewhere have existed for eons.

Writing in *Sky and Telescope*, Charles R. Pellegrino had this to say about meteoritic amino acids:

. . . some manner of preliving chemical evolution, perhaps advancing in the direction of molecules that would one day be able to reproduce themselves, appears to be preserved or fossilized in meteorites.

These celestial vagrants offer the alluring possibility that the universe is not such a lonely place in which we live.

Clouds of formaldehyde spread across various parts of the galaxy seem to exemplify the trend: Wherever carbon and hydrogen and their associated counterparts lie scattered and heated at the right temperature, it is a fair bet that they will coalesce into compounds of higher order.

That you are alive and reading these words is evidence that such reactions can and do occur.

What to Think

A fascinating national survey taken recently showed that nearly half of all Americans believe that there is intelligent life on other planets. It also appears from the poll that the more intelligent the person, the more likely he or she is to accept the possibility that we are not alone; and the older we become, the more set we are in our ideas.

Younger and more educated people were more likely to believe in extraterrestrial life-forms than older and less educated people. About half of the eighteen-to-fifty-four-year-olds said they thought intelligent life existed on other planets, compared with 43 percent of the fifty-five-to-sixty-four-year-olds and one-quarter of the sixty-five-and-older group.

Fifty-two percent of college graduates believed in life on other planets, compared with only 27 percent of the high-school dropouts. Forty-five percent of high-school graduates said they believe other life exists in the universe.

The Media General–Associated Press poll showed that, overall, 47 percent of us believed alien life exists.

With the coming of Allende to the Zone of Silence, we have had to take a hard new look at the biblical versions of the origins of human life, the Garden of Eden, and Adam and Eve. And the origin of the species theories of naturalist Charles Darwin suddenly begin to take on a lot more credibility.

We not only have to rethink the formation of our own life on Earth, but to now look more closely at meteorites like Allende which scientifically reaffirm the possibility of life on other worlds.

Banderros Mountains. Pancho Villa's famed stronghold at the edge of the Zone.

Last outpost of civilization: Ceballos, the gateway to the Zone.

The plaque at the entrance to the Biospheric "secret" Laboratory in the heart of the Zone.

EL C. PRESIDENTE DE LA REPUBLICA
LIC. JOSE LOPEZ PORTILLO
INAUGURO ESTE LABORATORIO DE
INVESTIGACION CIENTIFICA EN LA
RESERVA DE LA BIOSFERA DE MAPIMI,
EL 5 DE JUNIO DE 1978
"AÑO DEL GENERAL FRANCISCO VILLA"

Don Rosendo (left) and Professor Harry de la Pena observe the wildlife in the "zoological" courtyard at the center of the Biospheric Laboratory.

Don "the Godfather" Rosendo, benefactor of the Biospheric Laboratory and owner of large tracts of land in the Zone.

Official U.S. military photo of an Athena missile blasting off.

At Torreon's unique museum dedicated to the anomalies of the Zone, Harry de la Pena points to a photograph of the Athena missile debris before removal from its crater. Surrounding photos also display the Athena crash site.

Left: A regular native North Mexican turtle. Right: A baby giant tortoise from the Zone, clearly showing the strange triangular or pyramidal dorsal segments of its shell. *(Photo courtesy of Dr. Luis Maeda)*

Experimental setup to display the strange magnetic properties of certain Zone rocks. Note: All three compass needles point (as expected) to magnetic polar north.

Once a Zone rock is positioned in the center, compass needles bizarrely swing away from magnetic north—in different directions!

As the rock is rotated, the needles yet again change positions to display even different readings.

Artist's rendition of Allende meteorite. *(Photo by permission of Harry de la Pena)*

Typical samples of meteorite found only in the Zone and displaying a vast array of peculiar and thought-provoking shapes.

A small chunk of the incredible Allende meteorite. Owned by Harry de la Pena, its value to science is incalculable. This one sample could be considered rarer than rock brought back from the moon. *(Photo by permission of Harry de la Pena)*

In many meteorite fields within the Zone, "nomads" in the millions litter the desert floor. The author, Gerry Hunt, collects samples.

Hunt (center) demonstrates radio blackouts for Dr. Luis Maeda's video camera. Looking on is Zone researcher Mia Flores.

Harry de la Pena searches for radio transmission "black holes" in the heart of the Zone.

Zone researchers (left to right): Dr. Sergio Flores, his wife Mia, and Harry de la Pena discover a strange pyramid-shaped artifact. Obviously man-made and a recent construction, it was probably put together as a religious or psychic symbol.

Fossilized giant seashell from the heart of the Zone. These types of finds were clear evidence that the Zone was once a vast ancient sea, probably linked to the Gulf of Mexico and the Bermuda Triangle.

An unexplained ancient man-made hill in the Zone. The transporting of thousands of tons of rocks to this site is a perplexing mystery.

The lynxlike carved statue discovered near San Ignacio Hill: Its origin, age, and the culture it came from are unknown.

A bizarre carved head (complete with turban or "aviator" headgear) found in the Zone. Like the lynx, its origin is part of the ongoing puzzle of the Zone.

Chapter 7

Bizarre Plants and Animals and More Surprises

ONE PUZZLE THAT has never been answered to the satisfaction of any botanist or biologist is the strangeness of the plants and animal life in the Zone.

It's difficult to comprehend that species which are so different could have evolved in one small area of the globe, while all around Mother Nature has stuck to more traditional rules.

And in some cases the freaks of nature actually exist alongside their perfectly normal counterparts.

Only in the Zone of Silence will you find red and purple cacti, and purple cactus trees, growing side by side with their more acceptably colored cousins in shades of green and brown.

Living exclusively in the Zone are the giant land tortoises that display pyramidal or triangular segments on their shells instead of the regular hexagonal shapes. They also have no tails. This remarkable species is not found anywhere else in the world.

Nowhere else will you find giant centipedes growing over a foot in length that have bizarre purple heads and tails and curious ring shapes forming their bodies.

A species of snake inhabiting the zone is perfectly white with piercing red eyes.

All these plants and animals have been observed, although many of them are still waiting to be officially cataloged in the annals of nature. And there are others of which little is known, even rarer animals which are said to exist only in the Zone.

Reports from residents near the Zone speak of a race of dwarf deer that inhabit the Zone whose peculiar stubby antlers can grow to the thickness of a man's forearm. Others tell of albino lizards, pure white with red eyes. Insects two and three times the size of their normal counterparts outside the Zone have also been observed.

There are no scientific explanations for why so many bizarre species of plants and animals should exist in such a small concentrated area. And there are no logical answers to the mystery either.

The only thing we can do is observe and wonder.

Curious Cacti

During a field trip to the Zone in 1986, the author was able to witness firsthand the unusual cacti.

And, just as Harry de la Pena had found on his first expedition to the desert area, a change to a pink hue can be seen on some roadside cacti on the outskirts of Ceballos, last outpost of civilization before entering the Zone.

As the Zone is penetrated farther the cacti take on a deeper red, and then finally turn purple in the heart of the Zone. The oddity is compounded by the fact that perfectly normal green cacti grow in harmony side by side with the strange ones.

The purple cactus trees are also no hallucination. Sprouting out of the desert and growing to heights of six or seven feet and more, their parched and brittle spiked branches take on a livid purple coloration. The expected norm would be browns and greens. But this is, after all, one of the strangest places on the earth.

Sectioning the purple and green cactus plants reveals that their internal biology is identical. Both species produce succulent green fibrous interiors. Only the skin pigment is different.

To date nobody has been able to offer an adequate botanical explanation for the bizarre purple cacti in the Zone of Silence. All the experts consulted by the author have literally scratched their heads in bewilderment.

There are theories, but most of the proposals, unlike the cacti, tend to not hold water for one reason or another. The following are ones that have been suggested:

The Zone has already been shown to act as a cosmic "window" which attracts increased extraterrestrial radiation. The purple plants are a result of this unnaturally high level of cosmic radiation. A purple pigmentation in the skin of the cacti may act as a protective shield. But if this is so, why aren't all the cacti in the Zone purple?

The "sunburn" theory. Purple skins are a natural evolutionary safeguard against increased solar radiation. Just as people receive sunburn and eventual tans by increasing levels of protective melanin pigmentation as a result of high levels of ultraviolet rays, so do the desert cacti. This could explain why the purple cacti change back to green when they are replanted outside the Zone. The problem with this theory is that again it doesn't explain the presence of ordinary green cacti in the Zone.

The Zone contains large amounts of magnetic rocks, geological freaks that have high iron content. A high incidence of ferrous oxides in the soil might lead to a reddish tinge in plantlife. Again, this theory dies because both green and purple cacti grow side by side in the same soil—and their green internal tissues show no signs of oxidant discoloration.

The purple cacti are evolutionary misfits, genetic mutations that grow in the Zone and in no other spot on the earth. But there is no logical explanation for why this should be so.

Possibly the strangest theory is that the purple mutants are a result of freak blasts of radiation of unknown origin and the desert plants have continued to proliferate as an independent species. An even stranger sidebar is that the source of radiation may be connected in some way with the high incidence of UFO reports from the Zone—possibly an unknown source of radiation that powers the extraterrestrial craft.

One factor has been shown conclusively: The cacti will lose their purple color when replanted outside the Zone!

Samples of both green and purple cacti were collected by the author and replanted outside the Zone in three separate locations. The green cacti continued to thrive unchanged.

But after three weeks the purple cacti had already begun to lose most of their vivid color, first changing to a faded purple, a light lilac in color, and then to almost white. As the weeks passed they began to take on a discernible green tinge.

Soil and climate changes may have been responsible for this effect, but the puzzle still remains. What causes them to grow purple in the first place?

Although there is no scientific rationale for the cacti, they are definitely not desert mirages. The bizarre purple plants and trees exist—and all anyone has to do to witness this phenomenon is make a trip to the Zone of Silence.

Strange Animals

The Zone's tortoises are of the species *Gopherus flavomarginatus,* an extremely rare breed of large shelled reptiles unique to the Chihuahua desert area of Mexico.

But the imponderable is why a subsection of this species, the tortoises that live only in the Zone, should be so different from their brothers in the deserts outside the Zone.

The giant tortoises, which can live to two hundred years, are not visible year-round. They sleep through the desert winter, hibernating from October to the end of March.

Their most obvious distinctions are the triangular segments that form the tortoises' dorsal shells. In every other species of tortoise on the earth the shell segments are hexagonal. At first glance the strange pyramid shapes on the shells clearly set the tortoises of the Zone apart.

But the mystery deepens. Instead of normal white cilia around the lens of the eye, the Zone tortoises have distinct yellow cilia. And the Zone species have no tails—an even more remarkable fact when one considers that these appendages are known to play an important function in the mating process!

A number of renowned experts were consulted for their explanations of the Zone tortoises, and they were baffled.

Dr. Richard Zweifel is curator of herpetology at the American Museum of Natural History in New York City, and he confirmed that *Gopherus flavomarginatus* is a distinct species of tortoise found only in northern Mexico. But of the bizarre anomalies among the Zone tortoises, he admitted, "There is something kind of strange about this whole thing. It sounds rather weird."

He added, "Quite honestly I've never heard of tortoises without tails and pyramid-shaped shell segments. I'd find it hard to believe they existed. All tortoises have small tails. To find them without tails is most surprising because they use them in mating."

Pat Burchfield is an adviser to the Mexican government on tortoise and reptile conservation programs, and, although not having examined a Zone tortoise, he admits that the species runs contrary to the normal tortoise population in northern Mexico.

Burchfield, curator of herpetology at the Gladys Porter Zoo in Brownsville, Texas, handles tortoises daily, and he's considered an expert on those from the desert regions of Mexico.

"Frankly, the type of tortoise you describe is extremely unusual. It is very rare. In fact, as far as I know, it shouldn't exist at all," says Burchfield.

But the reptile expert was willing to consider some strange possibilities when it was pointed out that other reptilian wildlife in the Zone displays albino tendencies, white skins and red eyes. Were the white snakes and lizards some form of genetic abnormality?

"I feel that may be the key," pondered Burchfield. "It's unusual to find an entire colony of albino animals, and even more so to discover other species in the same area to exhibit albino abnormalities. I would have to suggest that something in this area is causing genetic mutations.

"The whole thing is very strange. There must be something there in that particular area mutating the genetic makeup of lots of different animal life. There's something unusual going on that's affecting the chromosomes and causing the genetic compositions to change in these animals."

Another expert to concur with the speculation is Mike Davenport, supervisor of the reptile collection at the National Zoo's Department of Herpetology in Washington, D.C. "The collection of so many white-skinned reptiles in one small area is highly unusual. It does suggest something causing change at the genetic level."

Davenport added, "As far as I know, this must be the only place in the world where such a situation exists."

Zone researcher and cancer surgeon Dr. Luis Maeda is no stranger to observing mutant cells and the changes they enact on human tissues. After extensive studies of the Zone tortoises, he is convinced that the strange mutant plant and animal life could be the result of some unexplained form of radiation bombarding the area.

"What this radiation is and where it comes from is still a mystery," confirms Dr. Maeda. "From extensive samplings of different areas of the Zone with sensitive instrumentation, we are pretty sure it does not emanate from the ground, the rocks, or deep in the earth. The only other alternative is that it is extraterrestrial. And this further enforces the theory of the Zone being a cosmic window."

Dr. Maeda has even gone as far as to quantify the precise area in which the animal anomalies exist. The Zone tortoises only appear on the mysterious 27th parallel between meridians 104 and 106.

To see many of these wondrous animals one doesn't even actually have to endure going into the Zone. They are on display in the small museum dedicated to the Zone and founded by Dr. Maeda and Harry de la Pena in the Technological Institute in Torreon.

Also on display at the museum are hundreds of fossils which have been discovered in the Zone.

Desert Fish and Sea Snails

Finding sea fish and other marine life in one of the most arid desert regions on the planet is curious food for thought.

But it makes sense when the relics are fossils, the "wildlife" of the Zone eons ago when it was a primitive sea, and probably connected with the waters which now constitute the Gulf of Mexico and the fabled Bermuda Triangle.

When the Zone was the Sea of Thetis, almost 100 million years ago, it was a seabed thriving with marine life. Little is known of the strange fish life in the sea, although it's safe to assume that sharks were a dominant force and marine dinosaurs may have been in evidence.

As the earth developed and the continents shifted, the Sea of Thetis was literally left high and dry.

Ten years ago Dr. Maeda made a dramatic discovery: He found the first positive evidence that the Zone was once a sea.

Dr. Maeda found a fossil bank in the Zone that is littered with evidence of marine life. The scientist is obviously guarded about the exact position of the fossil field, but in 1986 he proudly displayed it to the author.

Deep in the Zone, not too far away from a large meteorite field, an unimposing hillside was to yield a wealth of ancient life. To the untrained eye the hill looks very much like any other, a mishmash of lifeless gray scattered rocks, cacti, and scrub brush.

"They are there. You will find fossils for yourself. Just look closely," Dr. Maeda urged. "Remember, they have been there for many millions of years. Take your time; they are not going anywhere."

The fossils are not buried. They lie on, and in, the surface of the desert dirt, but they are not obvious. After fifteen minutes of close scrutiny, the author was unable to find one single ancient artifact. Of course, it seemed natural that Dr. Maeda had previously removed the most obvious discoveries.

"You are not looking as closely as you should," reprimanded Dr. Maeda. And then he opened his hand and displayed a half-dozen small fossils he had just found during the author's fruitless search. He smiled when it was suggested that he might have brought them with him.

With the eye of a hawk, Dr. Maeda pointed his finger. "See, about seven inches from the heel of your boot, there possibly is a fossil." A small pale pinkish rock, not much bigger than a thumbnail, didn't look particularly significant. "Examine it," commanded Dr. Maeda.

Incredibly, only just discernible to the naked eye was the tiniest of starfish etched into the rock. Under a magnifying glass the baby starfish was revealed in detail, right down to the minute filaments and ridges on its five legs.

And then another, and another.

A large sea snail, a fossilized mussel, a small sea urchin, another mussel. They were all there; the trick was knowing what to look for.

Dr. Maeda beamed. "You will make an archaeologist yet!"

On closer examination the sea urchin, smaller than a quarter but bigger than a dime, was a prize. In beautifully preserved detail, dozens of tiny spores covered the surface of the fossil from where once its protective spines had bristled: an animal from the Zone that lived when man was merely an evolutionary dream!

There was no doubt about it, the original wildlife of this strange area survived in a primordial sea.

The most common of the fossils are sea snails turned to rock. And petrified mussels, known as "mule toes" because of their likeness to the shape of a mule's hoof.

Said Dr. Maeda, "I have tried to keep this fossil bank as pristine as possible. It has not been excavated. We have only removed the obvious ones from the surface. Who knows what wonders lie below?"

At the museum in Torreon, even more astonishing fossil finds from the Zone are on show. Giant curled sea snails the size of dinner plates are on display for all to see, and so are the fossilized imprints of large ancient fish.

The origins of the bizarre wildlife in the Zone were primitive sea creatures that roamed the gloom of a deep sea during the Inferior Cretaceous period of life on Earth.

A Big Surprise: Reviving Life from 90 Million Years Ago

Is it possible to revive million-year-old beasties?

That was the premise of the most unusual biological experiment ever to be performed on the Zone's "wildlife." Although it took place at a microscopic level, it raises some awesome issues. Dr. Maeda, that eminent man of medicine, was actually able to bring back to life organisms that had been "dead" for at least 90 million years.

This new Zone twist on tales of science fiction was performed after Dr. Maeda and colleagues found minute spores in crystals of salt—accurately dated from their position in geological strata—that were deposited 90 million years previously. What had been locked in the crystalline formation of the salts from the Zone had remained untouched for an eternity, even since before the dawning of man. Yet it was to incredibly spring back to life in a culture dish in Dr. Maeda's hospital laboratory.

Dr. Maeda is cautious to point out that the experiment was not an attempt to "play God" and the result was entirely unexpected.

"Under the microscope we recognized that the spores might reveal a presence of former biological life. It was indeed of interest to us to discover what this might have been," explains Dr. Maeda.

The crystals containing the spores were carefully separated and inserted into a culture medium and kept under totally sterile conditions for the next three days at a controlled constant temperature of thirty-seven degrees centigrade.

The scientists, knowing that spores, much like plant seeds, can survive vast expanses of time in a dormant stage without germination, were interested to see if they could be revived.

Then the unexpected happened.

Instead of germinating, the minuscule spores produced a colony of active bacteria, bacteria that hadn't seen the light of day for millennia.

The germs were identified as a form of *Streptococcus viridaus*, a virulent organism that is the cause of many human health ills and infections; ancient germs from times before Homo sapiens even walked on the earth.

This discovery from the Zone of Silence was to stir profound thoughts in the minds of the astonished scientists. If it were possible to "awaken" bacteria from millions of years of "sleep," could this finding help in present medical research in the never-ending war against germs which are able to build up immunities to our ever-growing arsenal of antibiotics? Could these age-old forerunners of present-day germs offer keys to help us understand how bacteria build their defenses?

The seeds for future research were firmly planted.

But Dr. Maeda was not convinced that the bacteria were not a spurious phenomenon, possibly produced by a contaminated petri dish or culture.

The experiment was repeated with more spores from the salt crystals, yet this time other bacteria were also inserted into the culture at different positions in the dish to act as controls. One of the purposely introduced bacteria was a present-day version of the *Streptococcus* germ.

The control bacteria formed colonies, as expected, in the exact spots that they were placed on the culture dish.

And once more the spores produced their own easily identifiable and separate colony of bacteria.

What followed next was an elemental test, profound in
its simplicity, which aided in confirming the scientists'
belief that they had indeed managed to revive one of the
earliest-ever forms of life.

When the powerful antibiotic penicillin was introduced
to samples from the cultures, the modern germs—including
present-day *Streptococcus*—showed an expected small per-
centage of survival rate depending on their predictable
resistance to the drug.

The ancient germs, without the benefit of any acquired
defenses against the penicillin, were completely, and totally, wiped out!

Dr. Maeda takes a philosophical view of the unusual
experiment. "The Zone of Silence not only presents us
with many unexplained plant and animal curiosities, in this
case it also gave us intriguing food for thought."

Chapter 8

Zone Folk

THERE'S NO DOUBT that the native people living around the Zone of Silence are a hardy race. They have to be to withstand the rigors of a parched desert existence.

But there's tough and tougher. Being tougher is having the ability to take a thick leather belt and bite straight through it.

This remarkable feat was performed in front of Dr. Luis Maeda by a lifelong Zone resident, and a septuagenarian at that!

"I'd never quite seen anything like it," admits Dr. Maeda. "I had long been interested in the different physical qualities exhibited by the people who live around the Zone of Silence. But this was unexpected."

The scientist was visiting the old man and his family as part of a study to analyze blood samples from the small population living in scattered outposts on the fringes of the Zone. One point always to fascinate Maeda was the remarkable state of superior dental health displayed by "Zone folk."

People living around the Zone live a desolate life. The

population of the states of Durango, Chihuahua, and Coahuila, which come together in the Zone, averages nineteen persons per square mile. In and around the Zone, the population averages one person for every twelve square miles.

In this impoverished part of the world malnutrition is a great worry. The people of the Zone eat meat no more than twice a month, survive mostly on vegetables they grow themselves, and drink unpurified water that has either been collected during the brief rainy season or comes from remote wells.

Yet their general good health is not only remarkable but a small wonder—and their teeth could come straight out of the front office of any reputable Hollywood dentist.

Of the many physical things that are lacking among the general population of northern Mexico, the most noticeable is teeth. Almost every elderly person is reduced to a mouth containing one or two brown stumps. Most Mexicans, both men and women, have lost the majority of their dentition by middle age, and the problem of lost teeth among young children is getting worse, not better.

Poor eating habits and malnutrition are blamed as the prime factors for the lost teeth and disastrous dental health. Around the Zone of Silence, conditions of nutrition are, if anything, worse than average.

But, unlike the rest of the population, the people of the Zone have million-dollar smiles.

"Their teeth are large, strong, white, and show little signs of decay," confirms Dr. Maeda. "It is not unusual for the people of the Zone to display full sets of teeth well into their seventies and eighties. This is a remarkable fact considering the terrible state of dental health observed in the general population.

"It seems to be a true anomaly because lifelong inhabitants of the Zone area do not appear to have nutritional habits that differ from the general population. If anything, they might even be getting less calcium and other essential nutrients responsible for strong teeth and bone structure.''

And to prove the point, Dr. Maeda related the story of the old man and the belt.

''I had called on the family in their outlying home near Ceballos to collect blood samples for a hematological study. The old man of the family was seventy-three years old, and as our range on the blood samples was males between the ages of sixteen and sixty, he may have felt a little ignored.

''However, I had remarked on the wonderful set of teeth he still displayed despite his age. Whereupon the old man took a heavy leather belt from a shelf, held it up to show me its thickness, and then bit straight through it.

''He didn't even need to chomp away at it. In one swift action he bit straight through the belt and, with a smile, handed me the two pieces to examine.''

Early Forefathers

The people of the Zone are descended from native Indian and Spanish stock. As Dr. Maeda puts it: ''On the anthropological scale the inhabitants of this area are a cross of indigenous with Spanish. They are a very dark-skinned people with an average height of 1.68 meters.''

The swarthy Zone folk are small in stature, at around five feet five inches, and their rough-hewn facial features with broad cheekbones are reminiscent of Aztec or Mayan Indians. Their deep mahogany skins can verge almost to the black scale, and their brown eyes are almond-shaped. Muscle structure is inevitably taut and sinewy, with no excess of fat, a biophysical structure well attuned to the rugged desert life.

Little is known about their early forefathers, although

for centuries the natives of the Zone have been mainly shepherds, crisscrossing the parched moonlike landscape seeking out patches of scratchy grazing land for their scrawny goats and cows.

But two products of human origin reveal that early Zone man had an artistic bent. Discovered in the Zone, and now in the trust of the museum in Torreon that is dedicated to the Zone, the two artifacts are stone carvings.

The first was discovered in 1970 by Captain Jaime Gonzales Sepulveda during the search for the ill-fated Athena rocket remains. While the intrepid Mexican army officer was scouring a small hillside east of Ceballos he stumbled over a softball-sized rock which appeared to display the face of a man.

Dr. Maeda, cocurator of the museum, describes the fascinating carving:

"It has been cut from basaltic rock indigenous to the area. The piece measures nine centimeters by ten centimeters. The head appears to be that of an Indian chief with characteristics very similar to the Indians of northern Mexico. The nose is Roman, the eyes are almost almond-shaped, the cheekbones are high, the lips are thin, and the chin is of regular proportions.

"The figure is wearing a turban over his forehead and touching his eyebrows. Upon rubbing the figure you can just barely discern that it was painted with a bright metallic pigment."

But the carving has also raised controversy from the von Daniken school of "ancient astronaut" thinking.

The so-called turban or headdress, as described by Dr. Maeda, has been likened to the style of helmet worn by our present-day space venturers. It's stretching a point, and the nearest this author would venture toward aviation headgear would be to say it may look similar to the leather skullcaps worn by the pioneering air warriors of World War I.

No dating has been made of the intriguing carving, as there were no reference points at its site to indicate any human habitation, and nothing like it has been discovered in the immediate area to indicate a particular native style or design. Its exact period in history may well remain an archaeological mystery; it could be a hundred years old, it may even be thousands of years old.

One clue to its antiquity, and the origins of its carver's race and his ancient connections with the Zone, may be revealed by spectroscopic analysis of the traces of metallike pigments on its surface. Samples are now being analyzed.

The second artifact to be discovered recently is less surprising because of its uncanny resemblance to the native ocelots and jaguars of the area. The carving in porous volcanic rock is twenty-four centimeters long and five centimeters high and is clearly meant to portray a feline figure.

Other archaeological findings in the Zone include water jars and pots fashioned from clay and ceramic, some very rough and rudimentary, while others show delicate handwork with painted designs.

Dr. Maeda comments, "These findings are interesting, as it would lead us to believe that the Indians of the northern Mexico region were not necessarily the uncouth food-gathering nomads we have been led to believe they were. Evidently they had some artistic sense and even more stability than we have previously given them credit for."

And the findings may act as pointers toward the theory that the Zone might once have been a thriving ancient metropolis, as alluded to earlier in this work, which suddenly and mysteriously died like the ancient cities of Ur,

Persepolis, and Mohenjo-Daro, all brothers on the 27th parallel, only to be covered by the shifting sands of time.

As for evidence of ancient astronauts, we'll probe exciting new speculations in a later chapter.

Zone Life

The total population of Zone folk is believed to be less than two hundred in probably no more than a dozen families. But exact figures are almost impossible to obtain because in this fifteen-hundred-square-mile area of strangeness there may be pockets of human inhabitants that are yet to be discovered.

It has even been suggested by more than one serious anthropologist that the Zone, because of its uncharted remoteness, may contain a "family" of primitive Stone Age people who have never been exposed to the modern-day wonders of the "outside" world: the Mexican version of the fabled Himalayan yeti (also on the mysterious 27th parallel) or the North American bigfoot. This, however, is highly speculative, but the reader will discover in the next chapter a first-person account of a bizarre encounter with a huge manlike beast in the Zone, which has been verified by several witnesses.

For the Zone folk a meager income is sustained by raising bony-backed cattle, far inferior to the more fattened beasts on the professional ranches in the area. A sideline is candle making. For centuries the people of the Zone have been producing candles from a little-known cactus plant that grows wild in the desert. Some families raise the cactus in scrubby gardens behind their adobe huts, or they collect it from the Zone. When the cactus is "bled" it releases a white milky mixture which hardens into a tallowlike substance. This oily natural plant "fat" is then molded with wicks to form a long and clean-burning candle.

The people of the Zone live in adobe huts, constructed from clay bricks which they make themselves and bake hard under the desert sun. The average home measures about twenty by fifteen feet, and in this single-story environment a family of three or even four generations may live packed together, sleeping two and three to a bed. The primitive dirt-floor homes of the Zone have little or no sanitation facilities, and many folk will take a once-weekly trip to communal municipal bathhouses in the nearest town.

To walk into a typical home around the Zone is to enter a twilight world of primitive bliss. There is no electricity, gas, or running water. The windows are small or don't exist at all, and the cramped interior reeks of the musky-smoke smell of the cactus candles.

Furniture is multifunctional, with beds doubling as daytime sofas or seats. Kitchen, living quarters, and bedrooms are combined in one open-plan room. A curtain of brightly colored coarse woven fabric may designate the sleeping quarters of the head of the household and his wife.

The focal point of the home is the communal eating table where meals are both prepared and served. Clay pots and jugs line rough-cut wooden shelves and contain the necessities of life, including dried fruits and herbs, salts, soaps, and the occasional measure of wine or native liquor.

Foods are cooked over an open fire grate, and pots are always on the boil or simmering ready to accept new ingredients. Without refrigeration, the best way to preserve fresh foods and the meager supplies of meat is to keep them constantly "cooking" at temperatures that defy the proliferation of bacteria.

Overall, home life in the Zone is a Spartan existence.

Outside the adobe shack, twigs and sticks bound together in tight vertical bundles to form a lattice make up the walls for tiny yards where the barefoot children of the

Zone play in the dirt and dust with pet dogs, scrawny
roosters, and the inevitable families of pigs and goats.

Most of the children are illiterate, and will remain that
way throughout their lives. At most, two out of every ten
children may be expected to learn to read or write. The
rate of illiteracy in Mexico is probably the highest in
Western civilization, and in the Zone the chances of gaining any useful education drop dramatically.

Yet despite the deprivation of living quality, the Zone
folk are charming and hospitable: their home is your home
when you visit. Everything is shared, right down to the
last clay pitcher of brackish, evil-smelling drinking water.

A city slicker—even by Mexican standards—would do
well to survive a day or so in the crucifying conditions of
the searing daytime desert heat and subzero night temperatures. And then the diet, mainly of green vegetables and
almost lacking in any form of protein, would play havoc
with the normal human digestive system, not to mention
the diversity of microbial and parasitic life which is ram-
pant throughout the available water supplies.

But their gritty desert-smart life-style has made them a
breed apart, hardier and tougher than the people living in
the comparative comfort of the nearby one-cantina towns.

And Dr. Maeda discovered that this superior quality of
survival against the odds showed up in the makeup of the
blood of the Zone folk.

Hematological Studies

Dr. Maeda's interest in the inhabitants of the Zone
started in the mid-seventies when he tried to draw a correlation between the high incidence of certain cancers, especially skin cancers, and breast and uterine tumors in the
female population in the surrounding Laguna district of
Mexico.

Chemicals in the soils were pinpointed; so was the almost nonstop exposure to ultraviolet rays from the sun (it has been calculated that the sun shines brilliantly for 314 days a year in this region); and then, with the knowledge of suspected radiation anomalies in the Zone, there was the distinct possibility of yet another carcinogenic problem.

The surgeon made no scientific breakthroughs among the general population when he performed blood workups, except to confirm that the low-protein diets of the people in this poverty-stricken corner of Mexico made them all borderline anemic, and some seriously anemic.

But when he came to study the folk of the Zone he made a startling discovery—their blood counts displayed far healthier profiles than those of their surrounding countrymen.

Random blood samples were taken from 23 percent of the Zone populace, all males between the ages of fourteen and sixty, with a median age of twenty-eight years.

The first shock was in the discovery that not only were Zone folk not as anemic as their brothers on the ''outside,'' but their blood contained higher amounts of essential iron, a nutrient normally associated with a diet high in meat and animal products. And this surprise was discovered in people who eat meat less than twice a month.

The average hemoglobin content of the blood taken from the Zone folk was significantly higher than that of the general population. Hemoglobin is the iron-containing protein content of red blood cells. For the Zone folk it measured 15.2 grams per 100 milliliters of blood. An average for the normal population was assessed at 10.5 grams.

''Clearly something must account for this anomaly. But we could not pinpoint it,'' admits Dr. Maeda.

The surgeon and scientist continued: ''An extensive analysis has been conducted on the water these people consume, and there are absolutely no traces of iron in it. Many think that this iron anomaly has something to do with the natural iron occurring in the soil, and perhaps their source of unusual levels of iron lies in the vegetables and herbs that they eat. Another theory is that the iron is a result of increased cosmic radiation. It is possible that they could build up high levels of iron in the bone marrow. We do not know for sure.''

The Zone folk also displayed no noticeable deficiencies in their red blood cell counts, unlike the general population. In fact, both red and white blood cell counts far exceeded the accepted local norm.

These facts could explain the superior overall health of the Zone folk, both in quality and quantity of the oxygen-carrying red blood cells and the white cells so crucial for immunity and fighting off illness and disease.

The average red blood cell count for the Zone males was 5,300,000 per cubic millimeter. By comparison the population of the Laguna region show averages well below this level, with many around 3,500,000 per cubic millimeter, a fact that classes them as severely anemic.

And white blood cell, leukocyte, counts averaged 5,346 cells per cubic millimeter, compared to the general population figures of between 4,000 and 5,000.

''We honestly have no answers as to why this should be so in such a small isolated population of people. If anything, their diet is inferior to the general population, and their blood counts would be expected to reflect this malnutrition. Yet it doesn't,'' explains Dr. Maeda.

''The same blood tests were run on the people of the nearby Laguna district, and the differences between their readings and the readings from the Zone were obvious and significant. But we have no explanation. The people of the Zone are seemingly a biological mystery.''

The findings of Dr. Maeda's intriguing blood samplings were reviewed in the U.S. for the author by medical scientist Dr. Emile Bliznakov, whose pioneering work with cancer and immunobiology, together with medical colleagues at the New England Institute and the Yale School of Medicine, make him one of the foremost experts on the human body's health defenses.

Dr. Bliznakov was quick to point out, not surprisingly, that the blood findings as a whole were indicative of an extremely poorly nourished population. A red blood cell count in the region of 12 million per cubic millimeter was once accepted as "normal," but in recent years modern medical science has come to accept the figure of 8 million as more appropriate to the average U.S. population. Likewise a leukocyte count of 8,000 would be considered as within normal parameters.

"It is obvious from Dr. Maeda's findings that the population as a whole displays very low levels of red and white blood cell counts. This is an indication of a terribly malnourished people who show signs of severe anemia," commented Dr. Bliznakov.

He continued. "What I find extremely interesting, with consideration to the similarity in nutrition, is that one small section of the population could exhibit totally different blood readings. Nutrition should be the only deciding factor. But here it does not seem so.

"Other factors that might account for anomalous blood levels between two sections of the population eating essentially the same range of nutrients could include excesses of radiation. That cannot be discounted. But experience has taught us that higher levels of radiation, if anything, would be expected to result in reduced blood counts.

"Although we utilize radiation at many levels in modern medicine, it's usually as an antagonist to kill unwanted cells, like those of cancer. A source of beneficial radiation that would actually promote healthy cell propagation has yet to be discovered."

The anomaly of the blood readings from the Zone creates yet another tantalizing puzzle. If it is clearly not food supplies that give the Zone folk superior blood profiles, what else could?

Are the strange sources of radiation and magnetic anomalies known to exist in the Zone, and only in the Zone, keys to this human jigsaw puzzle?

Whatever the answer, there's no doubt that the people of the Zone are unique, not only in their hardy way of life in one of the world's most inhospitable spots, but also for their unusual, unexplainable physical makeup.

Chapter 9

The Godfather and the Secret Laboratory

HE APPEARED out of the swirling dust, a legend among the people who live around the Zone.

His skin was the color and texture of burnished copper, and as he strode forward his rolling gait told tales of years of life on horseback.

A flashed smile displayed a sparkling show of white, perfectly aligned teeth, a phenomenon in itself in this impoverished, undernourished part of the world.

The look could have been "the grin of deception," most favoritely portrayed by Hollywood filmmakers when they want to illustrate the "smile and stab you in the back" treachery of an archetypal Mexican bandit. But his brown eyes were warm.

By no means a giant of a man, but with the build of a bulldog, he stretched out his hand in a friendly gesture. The power of his iron fingers could have easily cracked walnuts.

No one single person commands more respect or fear among the desert people than this man. A monster, mad-man, tyrant, enforcer, a kindly but sinister man, and a generous benefactor. He's been called all of these and more.

Without doubt he is one of the more mysterious characters to be witnessed in the Zone of Silence.

This was Rosendo Aguilera, or simply Don Rosendo— the Godfather. The term "Don" is used as the ultimate in respect.

But the Godfather can be as unapproachable as he is sometimes elusive. Maybe it was more by luck than fortitude that the author was finally to meet Don Rosendo.

That he was expected to appear on horseback was just a mental aberration. The cloud of dust was the result of his arrival in a Ford Galaxie sedan, the Mexican equivalent of a luxury Cadillac. Here in the middle of the Zone of Silence.

Don Rosendo was alone. And that's probably the way he prefers it. He is known to be an intensely private person, and very few people have been able to get close to him, except perhaps for the two men who have each devoted twenty years of their lives to studying the mysteries of the desert homeland he so jealously protects against outsiders and change.

Harry de la Pena and Dr. Luis Maeda made the formal introductions. Don Rosendo hugged each one like a long-lost brother.

"You are indeed fortunate," whispered de la Pena. "Don Rosendo is here and he will talk with you."

The stories Don Rosendo was to relate about the Zone were to make the skin crawl.

Land Baron

Don Rosendo owns a good portion of the land which makes up the Zone of Silence. But ever since the Mexican Revolution people do not reveal exactly how much ground they have, whether it be useless desert or prime locations on the beachfront of Acapulco. And especially today when the government may commandeer your lands and turn them over to the starving populace. It's sufficient to say that Don Rosendo's holdings are in the thousands-of-acres range.

He has a number of ranches, but the main one is on the edge of the Zone a few kilometers from Ceballos. The Godfather keeps one room always ready for his personal use, while the others in the ranch have been turned over to his peons, or cowboys, who herd his cattle and horses through the Zone. Federal troops bring their horses to Don Rosendo's ranch for rest and recuperation during long marches into the lonely desert.

In Ceballos Don Rosendo keeps a modest home, totally in keeping with the style of the adobe homes of his neighbors. His third home is in Torreon, more a showplace, but still not pretentious.

Don Rosendo is a two-time president of the junta of the municipal government in Ceballos. But being a former mayor and a powerful land baron are not the only reasons why Don Rosendo is held in so much awe.

He is also the "wise one": the one who makes all the major decisions in the area. Don Rosendo is the common man's law and order in and around the Zone. His word can overrule the federal troops who police the area.

If you need a blessing for your son's or your daughter's marriage you go to Don Rosendo; have a land dispute, and Don Rosendo will resolve it; a family argument or a squabble with neighbors, consult Don Rosendo and he will mediate. No problem is too big or too small for the Godfather.

This tough Mexican, who could probably trace his roots through the ruthless likes of Pancho Villa's revolutionaries, the Spanish conquistadors, and back to the native desert Indians of northern Mexico, might be in his mid-fifties. He's not. In 1986 Don Rosendo was sixty-eight.

He came to the Zone to hand-build his empire when he was just twenty. And despite the ravages of nearly half a century of brutal desert living, Don Rosendo looks in the prime of his life.

There is a side of personal tragedy, however, that Don Rosendo never discusses. He's been married for most of his life, but has never been able to produce an offspring. When Don Rosendo dies, the legend goes with him.

Monster or Madman?

The tales about Don Rosendo abound in Ceballos and the far-flung villages around the Zone.

Harry de la Pena remembered well the tall stories he was told on his first expedition to the Zone. He had not yet set eyes on Don Rosendo, so his yarns were secondhand at best.

He recalled that Don Rosendo had supposedly been attacked by a humanlike monster in the Zone, but many people had told him Rosendo Aguilera was the true monster, a frighteningly evil man who stalked the Zone at night looking to pounce on unwary travelers, and maybe tear out their hearts and eat them.

Don Rosendo let out a huge roar.

"If I'm the monster of the Zone of Silence, then who attacked me that night? Answer me that!" He bellowed with laughter.

So, it was true. Don Rosendo experienced a bizarre happening in the Zone.

"It was something I cannot explain. But I had witnesses; three peons were camping with me that night. And they know I am not a man easily scared."

De la Pena and Dr. Maeda had warned that Don Rosendo

might be reluctant to recount his weird experiences in the Zone, especially to an outsider, and a gringo at that. But in this meeting Don Rosendo appeared to be in affable form.

"You want to know what happened. I'll tell you."

Don Rosendo was suddenly very serious. He explained in detail that he and the peons had been out in the desert checking fences, making repairs, and counting cattle. Night fell, and after tethering their horses they made camp.

It was after Don Rosendo had fallen into a peaceful sleep under the clear desert night sky that he was suddenly awoken by a great weight pressing upon him.

"I felt large hands around my neck. Somebody or something was trying to throttle the life out of me," Don Rosendo recalled unblinkingly.

"This thing was on top of me. It was pressing all the air out of my chest. I tried to pull the hands from my throat. They were cold, but very, very strong.

"I was struggling, gasping for breath, and I tried to cry out to my men. I knew I was not dreaming, because I could feel the great weight of this monster.

"I tried to roll it over on its back, but it was too big. I could feel the life draining from me, but I still struggled to get from under this thing. I don't remember much more. Maybe I passed out for a second or so.

"Suddenly the pressure on my throat eased. My men were with me. They had heard the disturbance and seen the shape of two bodies wrestling in the dust. Three of them were pulling the monster off.

"It threw them, all three of them, aside and began to run from the camp. I was on my feet now, and we gave chase.

"We could see its shadow getting away from us. It was a huge thing, bigger than a normal man, and it seemed to leap along, not run. We chased it to a clump of bushes, but it disappeared into the night.

"To this day I do not know if it was man or animal. But the marks on my throat and chest showed something very strong had attacked me."

At daybreak Don Rosendo and his cowboys scoured the entire area and the scrub brush for any telltale signs of their inhuman attacker. They found nothing, not even footprints in the soft dust.

There is even a bizarre postscript to this eerie story.

Some three months later, as they passed through the same camp spot in daylight, they came upon human remains nearby.

"He was no more than a skeleton, covered with rags," says Don Rosendo. "We took the pieces back with us."

The bleached bones were taken to Ceballos with respect. Nobody had been reported missing in the locality, and there was no possibility of identification.

"We gave him a Christian burial in the cemetery in Ceballos, whoever he was," added Don Rosendo.

Don Rosendo attaches no significance to link the two incidents. And possibly we shouldn't either. If there was a connection, Don Rosendo is not saying.

He was, however, eventually willing to reveal more strangeness from the Zone.

Benefactor

It might be easy to brush Don Rosendo aside as a crank. Possibly a man who has been far too long in the sun. But the respect he commands makes him the most powerful person in these wild parts. There's also much more to his tough, swarthy exterior than meets the eye.

Don Rosendo is an educated man. Mostly self-taught, he is one of the few people in this area who can both read and write, and conduct a highly articulate conversation. He is also a pilot.

The Godfather owns two planes, one single engine, one twin. And the sixty-eight-year-old pilots them himself, very expertly according to anyone who has flown with him.

He is also a man of conscience. He recently had a group of peons plow over one of his desert airstrips with deep ruts after he suspected it was being utilized by drug runners.

Don Rosendo also gave to the Mexican government the means to build a top-secret laboratory to study the strange anomalies of the Zone of Silence.

The Laboratory

It could be a mirage.

Sitting five kilometers from the base of San Ignacio Hill in the heart of the Zone is an ultramodern, fully equipped scientific laboratory.

A huge tower with a pyramid-shaped top looms up over the distant cacti; then a long single-story brick building under a dazzling white roof comes into view. Various brick-built outbuildings can be seen while you pass signs which warn that you are trespassing on very private property.

It is known as the Biospheric Laboratory and was Don Rosendo's gift to his people.

The Godfather donated hundreds of his acres for the laboratory to be built and for the scientists to have unlimited freedom in one of the most important parts of the Zone. The actual financing for the facilities was funded by the Mexican government and UNESCO—it was considered that important!

Officially opened on June 5, 1978, the laboratory had no less a dignitary than Jose Lopez Portillo, the president of Mexico, to officiate at the small private ceremony. He flew in by helicopter to the mysterious area.

At the president's right hand for the ribbon-cutting cere-

mony was Don Rosendo, considered the most respected
guest of honor next to the leader of his country.

A plaque at the entranceway to the laboratory's heavy
oak main doors reads:

EL C. PRESIDENTE DE LA REPUBLICA
LIC. JOSE LOPEZ PORTILLO
INAUGURO ESTE LABORATORIO DE
INVESTIGACION CIENTIFICA EN LA
RESERVA DE LA BIOSFERA DE MAPIMI
EL 5 DE JUNIO DE 1978
"ANO DEL GENERAL FRANCISCO VILLA"

It doesn't go without notice that the lab is dedicated to
the man who fought the entire Mexican army to a standstill
in these badlands he called home, and went on to become
"president" of the republic: General Francisco Villa—the
revolutionary Pancho Villa.

Nobody enters the laboratory without written permission
and a special pass from the government. The existence of
the laboratory itself is no secret to the people of the area,
but what goes on inside it is.

It is here that leading scientists from throughout the
world come by special invitation to study the bizarre phenomena of the Zone of Silence.

At least three Russian scientists are known to have spent
some weeks at the laboratory, including famed Soviet researcher Dr. Natalia Kostenko of Moscow University's
Geophysical Institute. Her visit was hush-hush, but during
one of his frequent expeditions into the Zone, Harry de la
Pena was to meet and speak with the scientist.

"A very gracious woman. She had come across the
globe to study the Zone. That was very impressive,"
recalls de la Pena. "Dr. Kostenko told me her main interest was in the strange plant and animal life. She admitted

she had never seen anything like it anywhere else in the world, and was anxious to report her findings back in the Soviet Union.

"She was a little guarded. At that time it was early in her stay at the laboratory and she said she had not yet reached any scientific conclusions."

De la Pena and Dr. Kostenko have communicated on a number of occasions since by mail, but the protocol of her country has not allowed the scientist to divulge her findings to the Western world.

Celebrity

At the laboratory Don Rosendo is a celebrity. And, in deference to his generous role in its inception, he is officially cast as the laboratory's "host" when new scientific crews arrive.

Even without passes and government approval, Don Rosendo has the power to admit anybody he wishes to the laboratory. And he was gracious enough to give the author an exclusive conducted tour during our 1986 meeting.

The first surprise the laboratory holds is an enormous rustic beamed meeting hall. It is complete with a long conference table, large enough to seat up to twenty people; deep padded couches and easy chairs; and a giant "walk-through" fireplace and chimney in the center of the room.

"It can get extremely cold at night and the fireplace is very cozy," explains Don Rosendo. "We like to make life in the middle of the desert a little more, shall we say, acceptable."

All the comforts of home in the middle of one of the strangest places on Earth!

Don Rosendo is obviously proud of "his" laboratory as he leads this visitor from room to room. A fully loaded modern kitchen feeds the intrepid scientists, and at least a quarter of the laboratory's twenty-odd rooms are given over to individual bedrooms and bathrooms decorated with typical native Mexican rugs and wall hangings.

Two main laboratories are equipped with stainless-steel workbenches, sinks, and blackboards. Everything is run by electricity supplied from the lab's own generator.

As Don Rosendo explains some charts and maps on the wall, a lab assistant comes to whisper in his ear.

"Ah, good," responds a delighted Godfather. "Come." He beckons. "You might want to see this. It will be like your July Fourth."

Don Rosendo leads the way out of the building and points to the sky.

"The French, they are making some tests," explains Don Rosendo."

Whooooosh!

Startlingly, from somewhere on the other side of the building a small missile whizzes into the air . . . one hundred . . . two hundred . . . three . . . possibly a thousand feet . . . and then it fizzles out—only to be replaced by a large parachute that rocks gently back down to earth.

"Something to do with testing the atmosphere." Don Rosendo beams. "But they don't tell me everything," he adds quickly before being asked for a detailed explanation.

The French scientists were tight-lipped. Nothing came about from the author's questioning except amiable smiles and a lot of good-natured shaking of heads. The French scientists had been at the lab for a month. They had planned their visit for some two to three years in advance. And they weren't about to reveal the nature of their carefully designed and orchestrated research to an outsider.

Whether by design or in response to top-secret orders, it appears that scientists performing experiments at the laboratory are not at liberty to talk about their work.

Enclosed on all four sides, but open to the skies, is a

picturesque Spanish-style courtyard in the middle of the lab. Red-tiled walkways and Moorish arches surround a large garden of cacti, shrubs, and small trees. A cool oasis in the middle of the searing desert heat, the garden is more than it first appears.

Look closely, and in the earth can be spied the entrance holes to the deep cool burrows made by giant land tortoises. Every once in a while one will stick its snout out and then crawl into the sun to forage some food from the garden.

The idea of this miniature wildlife preserve is to study the habits of the regular native tortoises, brought in from the outside world, to see how they adapt to life in the Zone, and to observe if they might evolve the strange pyramid shapes seen only on the shells of Zone tortoises.

Another unique side to the experiment is to discover if they will mate with the Zone tortoise and whether the strange mutations will be passed on to their offspring.

After his expertly conducted tour of the laboratory, a relaxed and smiling Don Rosendo is again willing to relate more of his experiences from the Zone.

Continuing Mysteries

Don Rosendo explains with great seriousness that he has always had an extreme reluctance to tell all he knows about the Zone of Silence. His one fear is that the outside world would ridicule his observations, and those of other serious ecologists and scientists.

"What we see in the Zone of Silence, many people may not believe. They may feel we are not to be trusted, that we exaggerate. But we have no reason to do this," Don Rosendo emphasizes.

His biggest fear is that the area will become a tourist trap, filled with oddballs and curiosity seekers.

"We do not want to see the desert destroyed. It is too fragile and too valuable. The desert ecology is very vulnerable."

Apart from his peons, Don Rosendo is one of the very few persons to spend time living in the Zone. And it is because of his close ties with its environment that Don Rosendo is himself considered an expert on the wildlife, the geophysical anomalies, and the strange lights and UFOs known to frequent the Zone.

Don Rosendo pulls a chair up to the long conference table in the lab's great hall and pauses for thought.

It was unexpected that he would respond to questions about the high frequency of UFO sightings in and around the Zone. In the past, Harry de la Pena had likened it to pulling teeth. Strange unexplained flying objects are not on the top ten of Don Rosendo's favorite subjects. Being an aviator himself, he is reluctant to besmirch his image as a sane and experienced pilot with wild talk about UFOs.

But it was explained to Don Rosendo that, certainly in the U.S., pilots are considered the most valuable and trustworthy witnesses of UFOs, because of their superior knowledge of aircraft, aeronautics, weather conditions, navigation, and, not least of all, flying the sky itself.

"As a young man I marveled at the strange lights that would appear around the desert and especially on San Ignacio Hill. I always wondered what they truly were and where they came from," offered Don Rosendo.

Then, with a little caution, he continued.

"I have often seen the so-called UFOs. They are not an unusual sight here.

"Many times my peons have ridden in to tell me about strange lights. Only recently some of my men reported witnessing a giant green ball of light. It was huge, bigger than a house, and it moved horizontally across San Ignacio Hill.

"They described it as luminous, very bright, and definitely green. They said it vanished into thin air, it went out like turning off an electric light."

A smile broke across Don Rosendo's serious face. "Now you should ask me if my men would lie to me, yes?"

A nod.

"Well, they'd be madmen to do that," he emphasized with a cutthroat gesture. No further word of explanation was necessary.

Tito Santibanes, a forty-five-year-old engineer and the "favorite nephew" of Don Rosendo, has been one of the closest people to the Godfather for over twenty-five years. They often make hunting trips together into the desert at night.

Santibanes had revealed that four years ago, during a hunting expedition, he and Don Rosendo had experienced their closest encounter with one of the "lights."

Recalled Santibanes: "It was about two A.M., and the sky was very dark. Don Rosendo and myself were sitting by our campfire. It was very quiet, only the sounds of the desert.

"Suddenly, above us was a huge bright light. We looked up, startled. It was blinding; we had to shield our eyes from it.

"We stood up, and all around us everything was bathed in an eerie blue light. What was more unbelievable was that the light was as bright as day and we could clearly see the whole desert lit up for miles around, all the plants and bushes. Even the very distant hills and mesas were visible in the light.

"I'm a grown man, but I'll admit I was scared. Don Rosendo said nothing. He stood and tried to peer upward to see where the light was coming from.

"I could see no airship, no spacecraft, no shape of anything. Only the piercing light. Then it went out, just like that," he said, snapping his fingers. "It was pitch black again. I don't know exactly how long it lasted, probably no more than five or six seconds."

While this story was being related Don Rosendo nodded his affirmation continually.

"What he told you, everything Tito said, is true," confirmed the Godfather.

But Don Rosendo was to reveal that not all sightings have taken place at night. He, and literally an army of men, had witnessed a strange metallic flying object come out of the sky and crash straight into the side of San Ignacio Hill.

"We saw the craft and we heard the impact. There was no doubt about it," admitted Don Rosendo.

The mysterious flying object was also witnessed by a regiment of federal soldiers who were resting over at Don Rosendo's ranch to feed and water their horses.

"I cannot estimate the size of the craft, but it was disk-shaped and definitely looked as if it was made from a shiny metal substance. It swooped low over the desert and then, for no apparent reason, it crashed straight into the side of San Ignacio," Don Rosendo said, slamming one giant fist into the palm of his other hand to emphasize the motion.

"I saw it, the soldiers saw it, we all saw it. At first we thought it might have been an aircraft, even though it didn't look like one. It was just before sundown, but immediately the soldiers rounded up their horses and set out as a rescue party.

"I drove to one of my airstrips and took the plane up. I was circling the hill within fifteen minutes of the crash, and I could see the soldiers in the foothills.

"I came in very close to where the craft crashed, but I could see no debris. There was no sign of fire or even impact. Nothing. I made a half-dozen more passes, but still I couldn't see anything, so I came in to land, thinking maybe the soldiers would find something.

"Three or four hours later, way after dark, the soldiers returned. They had also found nothing. It was a mystery. We were all puzzled and had no explanations.

"At daybreak the infantry took off yet again to search the hill but came back with nothing. They drew a complete blank. To this day we do not know what happened. We know something crashed into the hill, but when we got there it had vanished."

Don Rosendo is an astute man with sharp eyes. He also doesn't mince words.

"A blind man could have seen it," he exclaimed. "The way that thing crashed into San Ignacio you could hear and feel it. There was no doubt about it."

But Don Rosendo had kept back his most unlikely story for last, and he prefaced his tale with the forgiving attitude that if none of the listeners believed it, he wouldn't blame them.

Six years ago Don Rosendo and two of his cowboys were working on maintenance jobs around the laboratory when out of the early evening sky floated . . . a gigantic UFO mother ship.

"You may think this is crazy, but it happened, and we all saw it together," explains Don Rosendo.

"It was like looking up at a floating city in the sky. We were standing outside the laboratory, and this giant craft was moving very slowly east to west. It moved so slowly that it may have been hovering for a short time.

"There was absolutely no sound coming from it, and the noises of the desert seemed to die as well. It was like the quiet of the dead. Everything was silent.

"The entire craft seemed to glow with a bluish green haze, and it had lights running horizontally along it. They reminded me of looking down from my plane over a big city and seeing rows of streetlights.

"This thing was huge, bigger than anything I have ever seen in the air. It seemed to stretch from one end of the horizon to the other. It was so enormous that I had no point of visible reference by which to measure it. But it completely blocked from view the towering San Ignacio Hill, only five kilometers away.

"The ship looked like a giant football with a flattened bottom and top. At the rear of the craft, or what we assumed to be the rear of the craft from the direction in which it was traveling, there appeared to be vents or tubes—I don't know why, but they reminded me of escape tubes—and out of these also shone lights.

"You ask me, was I frightened? I didn't have time to be. I was so awestruck. I had never seen anything like this in my life.

"Very slowly this floating city edged toward the west, and then it was gone. Whether the lights went out, or it moved away with such speed, we could not tell. But in an instant it was no longer there."

Don Rosendo shuffled uneasily in his chair, and a pained quizzical expression came to his face.

"Now maybe you'll really think I'm a madman, eh?"

The one thing anybody knows after meeting Don Rosendo is that he's definitely no madman; neither is this rock-hard Mexican a man prone to flights of fantasy.

It was with great reluctance that Don Rosendo related his tales of the unexpected, and before leaving he politely requested that, however they were retold, he should not be made to look foolish.

The enigmatic Don Rosendo is not the only one to have had visions of fantastic voyagers in the Zone. There are many more who can attest to the presence of mysterious lights and bizarre flying objects in and around the Zone of Silence.

Chapter 10

Eerie Lights and UFOs

IT'S JUST AFTER twilight in the Zone of Silence. Far away across the uncluttered desert landscape the last orange breath of daylight forms a backdrop for the mesas, displaying them irregular and bold on the horizon. It's picture-postcard time in the Zone.

As the natural lumens fade even further, a trick of the imagination reveals a twinkle of light on the side of a distant mesa. A blink, a rub of the eyes, but the flicker is still there.

The night stars are clearly visible, but it appears that one of them has lost its hold on reality and fallen to the desert. Then another is spotted a little to its right, and yet one more slightly above. Fires maybe, now a series of them, four or even five. Somebody is out there, a small camping expedition.

No, the lights, now clearly visible bright yellow glows as the darkness descends, begin to move into a line. People with camping lights. But wait; these objects must be at least five or six miles away. Flashlights wouldn't have that penetration. And at that distance they must be

145

hundreds of feet, possibly yards, apart. Yet there they are lined up in precise formation on the sides of a high mesa which most probably has sheer vertical walls.

Impossible!

Now they begin to jiggle. They dance into an almost perfect triangle. The eyes are tired; staring too long has strained the optic nerve and the eye muscles; a slight tremble in the system of visual communication makes it just look as if they move. A normal optical illusion. But they stay in the triangle, not the straight line. Count them; now there are seven, no, eight! Then they blink out, vanish completely.

It was all a trick of the light. The brain had been fooled. Interesting, but obviously not too unusual. Time to call it a day.

Incredibly, there they are again, and this time on a different mesa, half the horizon away from the first, in the exact same geometric configuration! Not only impossible now, but ridiculous!

Suddenly they begin to separate and string out again. One shoots off to the west. It's out of the field of vision in less than a second. A truly phenomenal speed. Another drops toward the desert floor, hovers, splits into two, and both take off as a pair, vertically straight up, and are instantly lost in the myriad of genuine sky stars. The others pull together and form one, now orange-colored, ball. And then they are gone!

This bizarre phenomenon takes place regularly in the Zone.

The Zone's eerie lights have inspired both awe and fear in the populace, but no persons know them better than the night riders, hardened range hands who patrol the herds during the dark hours and see the glowing orbs most often.

These midnight cowboys are rattled by nothing in their wilderness environment. They understand little about UFOs and don't particularly care to. But they do know something about the strange lights buzzing the desert. What they know is that they are totally unexplainable and unpredictable.

They see them floating ghostlike up and down the sides of steep mesas, hovering in perfect regularity over their herds, and suddenly vanishing without trace, or zipping up to the heavens at incredible speeds. They are fully aware of the difference between the illumination of meteorites, which only comes down, and the bizarre lights which dance in the dark and even go up.

Literally hundreds of sightings have been reported in the Zone.

Pablo "Paco" Suarez, a twenty-two-year-old cowboy on a ranch bordering the Zone, had his first experience coming face to face with the UFO lights one night while guarding fences along with two other hands.

He recalled: "We saw a box-shaped group of lights hovering off toward the north, and very high. Then it began to drop lower and come toward us.

"There was a mesa in the distance, and this thing lowered behind it. We thought it had gone. Then it came around from behind the mesa, much lower than before, lower than I've ever seen the lights, and it started coming closer toward us.

"I admit I was scared. I sat frozen on my horse. Whatever this thing was, it kept coming toward the spot where we were, very slowly. I could see the lights were white and orange, and I think there was some yellow as well. They just kept coming.

"I turned to my friends to ask what they thought it was, but they too were staring silently at the sky. I don't think any one of us could speak, it seemed so unreal, not natural. I was about to turn my horse away when it suddenly disappeared about a quarter of a mile from us.

"My feeling was that it shot straight up in the air, but it

went so very fast that now I am not sure. I shivered and blinked, but they were no longer there.''

Paco had previously witnessed the lights at another spot within the Zone known as San Ignacio Hill. Locals frequently make reports of "the glowing ones" climbing up and down the hill, or hovering, only to vanish when search parties have attempted to pin them down.

"I have sat outside at night and watched the lights climb San Ignacio, but I have never wanted to investigate them. That is a dangerous, baffling place, and it is best not to go there.''

Search parties led by Rosendo Aguilera have more than once tried to identify the mysterious lights. But, like many others, their attempts ended in frustration.

Don Rosendo, the Godfather, explained, "Many times, I have seen strange lights climbing the sides of San Ignacio Hill. I used to watch them as a boy, and later as a young man.

"The lights would begin at the bottom of the hill, then the next light would ignite and the first would go out, and so on—a string of fifty lights making a continual pattern from the ground to the top. Finally, several years ago, I decided to see for myself what it was.

"I took a group of peons and we drove to the mountain to see what was happening. We stopped about a half mile from the mountain and began to walk toward it.

"All the way, I could see the lights climbing the side of the hill. But when we reached the base of the hill and started climbing, there was nothing to be seen. After searching for an hour or two we found nothing and left to return home.

"Turning around before we started back, I saw that the lights were back, only this time they were climbing the opposite side of the hill! We left anyway. I had had enough of that strange search.

"Yes, I still see the lights today. They are still there climbing the hill."

Dr. Hector Lopez-Loera, a professor of geophysics at the Department of Geophysical Science, National University, in Mexico City, has confirmed the existence of the lights through eyewitness reports from scores of people around the Zone.

"There is no doubt that these lights exist," confirms the scientist. "But what they are and where they come from is a mystery. Maybe they are UFOs, or from UFOs. I know that there have been several recorded sightings of strange flying objects in the Ceballos area."

Ceballos Chief of Police Chaparro has also witnessed the lights himself. "With my own eyes I have seen these lights in the sky. They are not meteorites, they dance around, very bright, white and red, and they tumble through the air.

"These might be UFOs; nobody knows for sure. People report them to me sometimes as lights, other times as UFOs. When it happens I make reports to the authorities in Durango. But they never send anyone to investigate. Maybe they think that so near the Zone, we are crazy people!"

While the bizarre lights of the Zone add an eerie touch to its many mysteries, and the residents around the Zone have grown blasé to their persistence, nocturnal lights are a genuine phenomenon. Most UFO experts agree it is one paranormal aspect to be seriously reckoned with and not to be taken lightly (no pun intended). There are some very good reasons—most of which inevitably turn out to lead directly back to solid "identifiable" UFOs.

Light phenomena are not unknown in UFO investigations. In fact, nocturnal lights which could be due to natural phenomena are the first things to be ruled out when taking UFO reports. These would include bright meteors, aircraft landing lights, balloons, planets, violently twinkling stars, searchlights, advertising lights on planes, refueling missions, and so forth. Most of these can instantly be discounted for the area of the Zone, especially when we consider that residents around the Zone are more than familiar with meteorite showers and the usual alignment of the commonly observable stars of the night sky.

The most numerous "genuine" reports of nocturnal lights are made by air control operators, commercial and private pilots, and police officers—all of whom could be considered accurate observers by virtue of their professions alone.

Inconclusive sightings by members of the public most often occur in built-up areas where a whole host of legitimate mistakes can take place, including distant streetlights, neon signs, advertising gimmicks, the reflection of nearby city lights from clouds or thermal heat inversions, and, of course, aircraft. The Zone of Silence doesn't have any of these confusions of modern society.

Dr. J. Allen Hynek, with whom this author has worked on numerous UFO investigations, is a severe critic of Project Blue Book (despite being a leading former member of its investigations panel and advisory committee) in its handling of the nocturnal-lights phenomena which was, for the most part, dismissed as "unusual but natural" events.

He does not underplay the significance of nocturnal lights—especially when there are no confusing backgrounds, and no logical reason for them being there—as in the Zone of Silence.

As an example of the official cavalier attitude toward mysterious lights, and why they should not be dismissed out of hand, Dr. Hynek, director of the Lindheimer Astronomical Research Center at Northwestern University in Evanston, Illinois, cites the "Midwest Flap" of August 1, 1965, when lights were observed over several states.

"Strange nocturnal lights were reported by ostensibly

reliable police officers on patrol at various places over an area of several hundred square miles. Blue Book dismissed this event as 'stars seen through inversion layers,' although I know of no astronomer who has ever witnessed inversion effects that produced these reported effects. Both past experience and calculations show that such illusory effects, in which stars move over a considerable arc of the sky, simply cannot be produced by thermal inversions.''

Dr. Hynek strikes back in the defense of all those civilians and police officers who witnessed the lights that memorable night. He exposes what was actually going on in the Blue Book control center at the very same time. His military revelations prove conclusively that there must have been more substance to the lights than the top brass was about to admit.

And they also vividly illustrate a crucial point about unexplained light phenomena—that what you see from the ground appearing as lights can take on a whole new UFO character of solid dimensions when viewed from the air.

What follows is an exact transcription obtained by Dr. Hynek. It is a Blue Book internal memo for the night of August 1, 1965, as recorded by Lieutenant Anspaugh, officer on duty for Blue Book.

1:30 A.M.—Captain Snelling, of the U.S. Air Force command post near Cheyenne, Wyoming, called to say that 15 to 20 phone calls had been received at the local radio station about a large circular object emitting several colors but no sound, sighted over the city. Two officers and one airman controller at the base reported that after being sighted directly over base operations, the object had begun to move rapidly to the northeast.

2:20 A.M.—Colonel Johnson, base commander of Francis E. Warren Air Force Base, near Cheyenne, Wyoming, called Dayton to say that the commanding officer at the Sioux Army Depot saw five objects at 1:45 A.M. and reported an alleged configuration of two UFOs previously reported over E site. At 1:49 A.M. members of E flight reportedly saw what appeared to be the same uniform reported at 1:48 A.M. by G flight. Two security teams were dispatched from E flight to investigate.

2:50 A.M.—Nine more UFOs were sighted, and at 3:35 A.M. Colonel Williams, commanding officer of the Sioux Army Depot, at Sydney, Nebraska, reported five UFOs going east.

3:20 A.M.—Seven UFOs reported east of site.

3:25 A.M.—E Site reported six UFOs stacked vertically.

3:27 A.M.—G-1 reported one ascending and at the same time, E-2 reported two additional UFOs had joined the seven for a total of nine.

3:28 A.M.—G-1 reported a UFO descending further, going east.

3:32 A.M.—The same site has a UFO climbing and leveling off.

3:40 A.M.—G Site reported one UFO at 70 degrees azimuth and one at 120 degrees. Three now came from the east, stacked vertically, passed through the other two with all five heading west.

4:00 A.M.—Colonel Johnson made another phone call to Dayton to say that at 4:00 A.M., Q flight reported nine UFOs in sight: four to the northwest, three to the northeast, and two over Cheyenne.

4:40 A.M.—Captain Howell, Air Force Command Post, called Dayton and Defense Intelligence Agency to report that a Strategic Air Command Team at Site H-2 at 3:00 A.M. reported a white oval UFO directly overhead. Later Strategic Air Command Post passed the following: Francis E. Warren Air Force Base reports (Site B-4 3:17 A.M.)—a UFO 90 miles east of Cheyenne at a high rate of speed and descending—oval and white with white lines on its sides and a flashing red light in its center moving east; reported to have landed 10 miles east of the site.

Hynek claims that when he confronted a "Major Quintanilla" of Blue Book with this evidence he was told that the sightings were "nothing but stars!"

The famed scientist and astronomer concludes, "This is certainly tantamount to saying that our Strategic Air Command, responsible for the defense of this country against major attacks from the air, was staffed by a notable set of incompetents who mistook twinkling stars for strange craft. These are the people who someday might have the responsibility for waging a nuclear war!"

In his book *The UFO Experience,* Dr. Hynek gives his interpretation of what constitutes a "genuine" light phenomenon:

> The typical Nocturnal Light is a bright light, generally not a point source, of intermediate linear size and of varying color but most usually yellowish orange, although no color of the spectrum has been consistently absent, which follows a path not ascribable to a balloon, aircraft, or other natural object and which often gives the appearance of intelligent action. The light gives no direct evidence of being attached to a solid body but presumably may be.
>
> As far as trajectories and kinematic behavior are concerned, despite exceptions that defy normal physical explanations, when generous allowance is made for exaggerations and error of judgment, the reported motions of the Nocturnal Lights do not generally violate physical laws.

The Zone's mysterious lights conform to all of the above parameters.

Military observers of one phenomenon on a single night in 1965 considered it important enough to be logged minute by minute. Imagine their consternation if they had to monitor the Zone of Silence on a daily basis!

"The Zone may be a home-from-home base for UFOs, a secure place from where they can disperse throughout the entire continent," suggests Professor de la Pena. "The regularity of reliable observations in the Zone is not to be sneered at. I agree with Dr. Hynek, much more serious emphasis must be placed on the study of unexplained nocturnal lights—until at least we know what we are dealing with!"

The Great Ceballos UFO

The great Ceballos UFO arrived without fanfare on a September evening in 1976. It was sometime between 9:00 and 10:00 P.M. when the first witness spotted the gargantuan craft hovering silently on the outskirts of town, and then moving almost directly overhead.

As word spread a group of some twenty residents collected on the main street to view the extraordinary spectacle. Foreboding and ominous, the great bulk of the craft just hung there. There were absolutely no engine sounds.

Various estimates put the craft at between one hundred and three hundred meters long. It was rectangular in shape, metallic, and may have had an oval roof, but this was almost impossible to view from the vantage point of most observers.

"I am certain it was rounded on top," swears Jesus Martinez. "I don't exactly know why, it just seemed that way, that it curved upward."

Pablo Hernandez remembers it differently. "It was flat

on top, and the top glowed. A sort of luminescence which might have made it look round."

What all the Ceballos witnesses agree on is that the craft was ringed with a series of lights on its outside edge. White, green, and blue lights were reported, the white being the most intense. The lights also seemed to "throb" or "pulsate" in a regular drone of soft humming sounds.

"It was like the rhythm of crickets in the night. But the noise was very low. You had to listen hard to hear it," says Martinez.

Another witness, Alicia Avalos, is sure she could feel vibrations from the noise. "I could feel something. It made the hair on my arms stand up on end."

Dogs began to howl in the streets of Ceballos, and their barking drowned out any other noise that could be sensed from the machine except by the closest observers.

The light from the object was intense enough to reflect from rooftops and cast an eerie phosphorescent glow across most of the town. There were no reports of spotlights, searchlights, or any form of illumination being beamed down directly at the ground.

"It was like we were being watched," recalls Ceballos's Mayor Silva. "After two or three minutes of this, people became very worried. They felt panic. This was a very frightening experience."

Estimates of how high the UFO was from the ground also vary, but most people seem to agree it was from thirty to fifty feet. At such a low altitude it would be almost impossible for ground observers to see anything but the bottom of the ship, unless they were some yards distant.

One witness, Jose Madero, claims to have seen the craft from approximately two hundred yards while standing next to a pigpen near his home. The elderly man recalled through an interpreter:

"I heard dogs howling in the street and my animals

making noise. The pigs were squealing, and I thought they were being attacked. There was nothing that I could see to worry them. But then in the distance, over the main street of town, I saw a huge dark shape in the air. It was sometime after nine at night.

"As I stood and watched it more closely I thought it was a big balloon. Like something you see at a carnival. But this thing was really big, I mean a giant. I could put my hand out at arm's length and it just about covered all of the object.

"It had lights around it. I only saw one string of lights, around the middle. They reflected off its skin. It looked like it was silver, possibly steel. I didn't know what to think. It was hanging in the air, not moving. I could hear no sounds. It was very silent.

"I was not afraid; I thought it was a joke of some sort. But I really didn't know what to think. I watched it for four or five minutes and then started to walk toward the center of town. Other people were coming out of their homes to see it. As I got nearer it started to rise up and head away from town toward the Zone. I heard no engines.

"People who were watching told me it was a UFO, a flying machine. I know what I saw. I do not know what it was. I have seen things like this before over the desert, but much farther away."

Police Chief Chaparro remembers that there was no overall panic, although some women and children were on the point of hysteria during the event.

"I think it best to say that most people were very curious. Some were scared, but most were interested to find out what type of flying machine this was. This was the first time anybody had seen a thing like this right over the town. I did not feel there was any danger to the people. I did not take any offensive action. It seemed peaceable.

"I made a report to authorities in Durango. But I heard nothing more."

Many theories have been proposed to show that flying saucers may contain power sources based on electromagnetics. We'll term this UFM—Unidentified Flying Magnetism. Magnetism is powerful, magnetism is clean . . . and magnetism is silent. How many people ever report noisy UFOs? Very few.

One of the most-often-pronounced conclusions by UFO researchers is that these unidentified flying craft emit little or no sound because they utilize a highly sophisticated power plant unlike anything we have yet developed on Earth. Most sightings are categorized by descriptions of low humming noises, whirrings, and swishing sounds, or nothing at all—but never the roar of a rocket engine! Our highly sophisticated jet engines may be as primitive as Stone Age tools by comparison.

The Ceballos incident fits many of the classic parameters associated with UFOs. But these reports from the edge of the Zone of Silence take on added credibility because most, if not all, were taken from people who have little education, are more likely than not to be illiterate, and have absolutely no experience of the high technology existing outside their primitive dimensions.

If these hardy desert folk fear one thing, it is ridicule. Poverty is a fact of life, but loss of face or reputation is the ultimate in humiliation to these proud people. They had a lot to lose and absolutely nothing to gain by making up fantasy stories about a flying machine they couldn't explain or comprehend.

The Ceballos UFO Fits the Pattern

As part of the U.S. Air Force's probe into UFOs, Project Blue Book—the most comprehensive study ever conducted by any government—the scientists involved came up with twelve classic UFO types and shapes, and assigned twelve real-life case histories to which best typified each one. To compile their dozen, 4,834 sightings reported to the Blue Book scientists were detailed on punch cards and fed into an IBM computer.

After the analysis, the UFO boffins found that 25 percent could be attributed to astronomical phenomena; 20 percent to conventional aircraft of all types; 16 percent to balloons; 13 percent to natural phenomena; and in 17 percent of cases there was insufficient information.

That left the experts with 9 percent of sightings for which there was no logical, scientific, or natural explanation. This group was officially termed Unknowns, and from it were derived the twelve UFO types.

The extraordinary significance of this classic dozen is the absolute lack of any audible or visible means of propulsion associated with most of them—and the reports of strange noises which mimic the sounds we might associate with magnetic energy.

Here are four of those remarkable actual case histories with their exact Blue Book descriptions (author's emphasis added), which illustrate typical sightings of UFOs appearing to have no conventional power source. The similarities between them and the Ceballos UFO are striking.

Case 1X (Serial 0066.00)

A farmer and his two sons, aged 8 and 10, were at his fishing camp on August 13, 1947. At about 1300 hours, he went to look for the boys, having sent them to the river for some tape from his boat. He noticed an object some 300 feet away, 75 feet above the ground. He saw it against the backdrop of the canyon wall which was 400 feet high at this point. It was hedge hopping, following the contours of the ground, was sky blue, about 20 feet in diameter and 10 feet thick. *It made a swishing sound*. The observer stated that the trees were highly agitated by the craft as it passed over. His sons also observed the object. No one saw the object for more than a few seconds.

Case X (Serial 1119.00)

An employee in the supersonic laboratory of an aeronautical laboratory, and some other employees of this lab, were by a river, 2½ miles from its mouth, when they saw an object. The time was about 1700 hours on May 24, 1949. The object was reflecting sunlight when observed by naked eye. However, he then looked at it with 8-power binoculars, at which time there was no glare. [Did glasses have filter?] It was of metallic construction and was seen with good enough resolution to show that the skin was dirty. It moved off in horizontal flight at a gradually increasing rate of speed, until it seemed to approach the speed of a jet before it disappeared. *No propulsion was apparent*. Time of observation was 2½ to 3 minutes.

Case XII (Serial 3601.00)

Description of the object is as follows:

It was about 75 feet long, 45 feet wide, and 15 feet thick, shaped like two oval meat platters placed together. It was a dull aluminum color, and had a smooth surface. A medium-blue continuous light shone through the one window in the front section. The head and shoulders of one man, sitting motionless, facing the forward edge of the object, were visible. In the midsection of the object were several windows extending from the top to the rear edge of the object; the midsection of the ship had a blue light which gradually changed to different shades. There was a large amount of activity and movement in the midsection that could not be identified as either human or mechanical, although it did have a regular pattern of movement. There were no windows, doors or portholes, vents, seams, etc., visible to the observer in the rear section of the object or under the object (viewed at time of ascent).

At 0535 on the morning of August 25, 1952, a musician for a radio station was driving to work from his home when he noticed an object hovering about 10 feet above a field near the road along which he was driving. As he came abreast of the object, he stopped his car and got out to watch. He was within about 100 yards of it at the point he was standing on the road. The object was absolutely still, but seemed to rock slightly as it hovered. When he turned off the motor of his car, *he could hear a deep throbbing sound coming from the object.* As he got out of the car, the object began a vertical ascent with a sound similar to "a large covey of quail starting to fly at one time." The object ascended vertically through broken clouds until out of sight. His view was not obscured by the clouds. The observer states that the vegetation was blown about by the object when it was near the ground.

Investigation of the area soon afterward showed some evidence of vegetation being blown around. An examination of grass and soil samples taken indicated nothing unusual. Reliability of the observer was considered good.

Case III (Serial 2013.00, 2014.00, and 2014.01)

Two tower operators sighted a light over a city airport at 2020 hours on January 20, 1951. Since a commercial plane was taking off at this time, the pilots were asked to investigate this light. They observed it at 2026 hours. According to them, it flew abreast of them at a greater radius as they made their climbing turn, during which time it blinked some lights which looked like running lights. While the observing plane was still in its climbing turn, the object made a turn toward the plane and flew across its nose. As the two men turned their heads to watch it, it instantly appeared on their other side flying in the same direction as they were flying, and then in 2 or 3 seconds it slipped under them, and they did not see it again. Total time of the observation was not stated. In appearance, it was like an airplane with a cigar shaped body and straight wings, somewhat larger than a B-29. *No engine nacelles were observed on the wings.*

Although the Ceballos UFO did not perform any extraordinary aerial gymnastics during its September visit, the numerous reports of nocturnal lights throughout the Zone attest to the incredible maneuverability of whatever craft perform them.

Here are some of the key points from eyewitness reports in Ceballos that mirror UFO guidelines for acceptability:

• The object was seen by numerous people from different angles.
• All witnesses reported the object to be huge in size and solid in shape—although exact estimates of its size vary, and this may depend on the angle of individual observation.
• Dogs howled in the streets. Yet another indication that the object was highly visible, solid, and not a mirage.
• Its skin surface was described by a number of witnesses as being metallic. Weather balloons may also give this impression, but would not generally fit further descriptions given by witnesses.
• No visible power sources were observed for the craft.
• It emitted a low hum which appeared to pulsate in frequency with the brightness of the lights surrounding the exterior of the object.

• The lights surrounding the object were described as white, blue, and green. Red lights are rarely described on UFOs.
• No spotlights were observed being shone down from the craft. Very few UFO incidents recorded as "genuine encounters" report high-intensity beams.
• Some witnesses reported being able to "feel" vibrations from the craft. The incidences of raised body hair—likened to a static-electricity effect—may indicate electromagnetic anomalies in the immediate vicinity of the craft.
• The machine was passive, as if in an observation mode.
• It hovered stationary without any observable or audible means of propulsion.
• The craft left the scene without warning with little or no air disturbance and no engine noise.
• No testings of military or civilian experimental craft were reported at the time of the incident.

Could it have been a helicopter? Hardly likely; the blast from its rotors would have been far too obvious, even for people who had never experienced a gyro machine. A Goodyear-type blimp? Anyone who has ever been seated in a sports stadium while a blimp is hovering overhead knows the tremendous racket kicked up by its propeller engines.

Only one conventional plane is able to duplicate the feats ascribed to the Ceballos UFO. This is the British-made Hawker-Harrier jump jet, a military VTOL (vertical takeoff and landing) jet which can soar through the sky, pull up to a standstill in midair, hover indefinitely, and land on a dime. It is, however, no bigger than an American F-16, and nowhere near the size of the Ceballos craft—and the roar from its twin Rolls-Royce jet engines alone would awaken the dead!

Of all the UFO reports gathered in the area of the Zone of Silence, the Ceballos enigma is the most outstanding, both from the number of independent witnesses and how tightly their observations correlate.

Nobody attempted to follow the craft. The direction of its departure put it heading toward the center of the Zone of Silence. Why it should have been hovering over Ceballos may forever remain a mystery.

Was it in the Zone for a magnetic refueling stop? Had it strayed from its planned course? Was the craft suffering technical difficulties? Or, if the ship did contain observers, were they just curious?

Chapter 11

Force Fields and Ancient Astronauts

WHY WOULD ANCIENT astronauts visit the Zone of Silence?

What is the force that makes the Zone so irresistible to UFOs?

What attracts millions of meteorites?

To examine these intriguing questions let's take a hypothetical viewpoint from far above the earth.

If you were to peer down at our planet from an alien spaceship for the first time, you might initially wonder at the array of fertile colors, the browns, greens, and blues, which distinguish it from other planets in this solar system. You check your star map of eternity to find out exactly where you are.

Earth would appear as an insignificant microscopic speck. The sun, just one of millions in a sea of stars called the Milky Way, might look like a microdot. This galaxy, in turn, possibly the size of a three-letter word, would be just one of many on the interstellar map.

On the general scale of things, finding Earth would be like picking out a single grain of sand on the seashore.

Your space mission is to discover new sources of energy. Nothing much about the colorful planet below gives any indication in this direction.

But, following your mission assignment, you sit there in your craft and begin to run some sample tests to determine a few more things about Planet Earth. Scanning devices show you that the major covering portion of blue is a sodium, hydrogen, and oxygen solution. The green parts are landmasses which give off massive amounts of carbon dioxide into the atmosphere. The brown areas seem less active, possibly dead zones. The whole system appears to be bathed in a bath of oxygen. It's an interesting-looking planet, possibly unique—but not exactly exploding in new sources of power.

In this scenario your on-board search-and-analyze program is linked directly to the brain by remote messages from your ship's main computer. No video screens are necessary; what comes out of the computer flashes into your brain's own visualization centers.

Then something rather extraordinary catches your mind's eye.

The computer scan is being performed by your spacecraft, which derives its intergalactic power from engines utilizing magnetic forces. You mentally request a quick rerun, and sure enough there are a couple of spots on the planet below you which exude magnetism.

One of them, a white area on the surface, looks inhospitable, being covered by a hard layer of crystallized oxygen and hydrogen. But the other, more central on your view of the planet's surface, looks inviting. Time for a closer look.

You are now descending to the Zone of Silence—one of the richest sources of magnetism on Planet Earth, possibly even stronger than the North Pole.

Our scenario is theoretical, but what on Earth could possibly attract such a multitude of UFO sightings, and so many millions of meteorites? Are they drawn to a gigantic magnet?

Although we learn about elementary magnetism in school, its importance as a dramatic new source of propulsion is only just now being appreciated.

The linear accelerator at the University of California at Berkeley is powered by principles of magnetism. Charged particles are accelerated on a straight line at phenomenal speeds by successive impulses from a series of electric fields. The fastest experimental train in the world runs on rails which utilize the attraction/repulsion mechanics of magnetism to ''fly'' it along at breathtaking speeds. Magnetics could be the new future of energy and motion.

Is it possible that advanced civilizations from other galaxies have already far surpassed our knowledge of magnetic potential?

It's well worth remembering that it's the whole principle of magnetism that keeps our universe intact. Without the attraction/repulsion of great masses our worlds might collapse into one gigantic hole—a void of antigravity.

Like the great Ceballos UFO and the classic examples from Project Blue Book, noiseless UFOs further reinforce the theories that whatever powers the craft of these supposed visitors to Earth, it is nothing that we recognize. Is magnetics the answer?

The magnetic anomalies of the Zone of Silence have now been repeatedly well recorded since Professor Harry de la Pena made his discoveries in 1966. And now more Mexican scientists are becoming convinced that this phenomenon may be a source of attraction for UFOs.

De la Pena offers the thought-provoking theory that if extraterrestrial craft do exist, and indeed if they use magnetism as a power source, it would be natural for them to be drawn to the Zone's powerful magnetic fields.

As we have to recharge batteries, take our automobiles

and aircraft in for regular servicing, and continually fill them up with fuel to keep them working, it's not too hard to understand that a UFO might be in need of a magnetic fix. On the intergalactic scale it would be extremely useful to have "servicing" or "refueling" planets available where sources of magnetism are readily available to be drawn from.

"It's only a theory, but it begins to make a lot of sense when you consider the magnetic wealth contained in the Zone of Silence," says de la Pena.

A Magnetic Meteor?

There is no doubt that the Zone's powerful magnetic fields do exist. But how did they get there? Are they natural phenomena—or were they planted?

One theory which tries to explain the source for the magnetism proposes it to be meteoritic in origin. Eons ago a giant meteor collided with the earth and blasted deep into the Zone of Silence. This space behemoth, hundreds of times the size of Allende, had an exceptionally high iron content. The ferrous metals may have been magnetic in origin, or they became highly magnetized during their light-years through space. Today, buried deep under the desert, it continues to radiate its magnetism.

But if such a cataclysmic episode had happened during the earth's early history, wouldn't there be evidence of a massive impact crater in the Zone? A meteor weighing many tons would hit prehistoric Mexico like an atomic bomb. Smashing into the earth at such a velocity, its sheer impact would cause an explosion of energy on an awesome scale. It would not only totally destroy most of the great bulk of the meteorite, but also displace millions of tons of the earth's surface which would fall back in and bury any remnants.

We know there is no trace of an impact crater, one that could be expected to be many miles in diameter. So the theory just doesn't make sense. Or does it?

If we consider that the same meteor hit the Zone of Silence when it was the Sea of Thetis, the great Cretaceous sea, an entirely different scenario could have evolved.

The meteor would have smacked into the sea with such force that the ocean would have erupted in steam. As it plunged through the depths its velocity would have been drastically reduced, its major energy dissipated into the boiling caldron surrounding it. It could have hit the seabed with sufficient force to bury it completely. Next, the seas of time would have washed over the impact zone, obliterating any trace of the great meteor before the entire area eventually evaporated to form the dehydrated desert it is today.

Even more way-out is the theory that suggests a meteor might have been purposely directed toward Earth by some intelligence within the universe.

The magnetism of the meteor, now safely embedded within the earth on our planet's highly predictable orbit, would make it an ideal "staging post" for intergalactic travel. Farfetched? Yes, but so is the Zone of Silence.

Scientific Curiosity

When scientists first heard about the magnetic anomalies of the Zone, through respected researchers like Harry de la Pena, they were initially skeptical.

This was hardly surprising, as de la Pena had already brought home readings which showed the magnetism pull in sections of the Zone to be greater than the pull of the North Pole. This was a fantastic finding, a phenomenon which would obviously make nonsense of any compass readings in the area, and there was also an initial suggestion that something had an equally strange effect on radio receptions and transmissions.

Transportation workers who had driven through the Zone had been talking about these bizarre force fields for years. But their reports had never been taken seriously by the scientific community.

Then individual scientists and even universities decided to try and find out for themselves.

A significant turn in events happened in April 1973 when the Geophysical Institute of the National University of Mexico made discreet inquiries of de la Pena in an attempt to discover what the heck was going on in the Zone of Silence.

The letter, signed by Dr. Adolfo Orozio Torres of the Department of Special Research, reads:

> We have some confusing rumors about the anomalies existing in the Ceballos region. In relation to the fall of the Athena missile of the U.S., we know that visitors come from American universities very often. But we know of no official scientific project under way, either Mexican-American or exclusively American.
>
> In fact, it is common knowledge that the scientific activities actually happen, and we consider that an activity of such importance must be known by the interested groups or in case of other kinds of problems there should be collaborations to solve the problem.
>
> We ask and beg you to inform us immediately what is happening and you will be sure that this information will be treated as confidential and top secret.

Magnetic Tests

Dr. Jacinto Meritano, professor of geophysical science and an aerial satellite photography specialist, was one of the early doubting Thomases.

"It was very difficult to believe at first," admits Dr. Meritano. "But I recall the first time the university sent a research team in to carry out fieldwork in the Zone. Radio contact with them was established, but then strange things began to happen.

"It was soon discovered that they could not be reached at all by radio in certain locations. This is what caused a lot of early interest, because it could not be explained.

"And this is why it first was called the Zone of Silence."

Other astonished scientists followed suit into the Zone to try to disprove the many different bizarre claims about the area. They were all unsuccessful.

One of the first converts was Dr. Miguel Carrasco, a geologist and engineer from the Technological Institute of Durango. His original intention, before becoming involved in the Zone's mysteries, was to survey the area for mineral deposits. To this end his first searches were fruitless, but the scientist was staggered at the wealth of fascination he found in the Zone.

Dr. Carrasco explained: "On one of my first trips out there, about eleven years ago, I found many meteorites which had fallen from the sky. In addition, I found a tremendous amount of fossils, including mammoth fossils.

"I became strangely drawn to the place. It has a wealth of interest and anomaly. Definitely, there is something very unique and mysterious about it. I feel the whole area is some sort of magnetic attracting zone on the earth, like a window to the stars. The area draws meteorites like a magnet.

"It reminded me very much of the Bermuda Triangle. Strange things happen there.

"I remember the first time I took a radio with me, I was astonished. In some areas I could get reception, but in other areas, only a few yards away, the signals suddenly died. It was as if an enormous unseen wall of lead had been erected to shield out transmission.

"Then I noticed a definite interruption in my compass when I was working in the areas of silence. The needle would just spin around, or not move at all. My watch also stopped. I knew that there must be some very strong magnetic attraction in that area to do these things.

"The Zone is a complete mystery, and we really don't know why these things happen. I have visited there six times in the past eleven years. Because of the radio problems, I suspected that a form of radioactivity might have been involved. I took an expert once, a fellow researcher who had equipment to detect radioactivity, but we found absolutely no trace. It is a very strange piece of the earth."

Mexico's huge National University soon founded an ongoing study to investigate the Zone of Silence. It started in 1977.

Dr. Tomas Gonzalez-Moran, a professor of geophysics, was one of the first university investigators, and is also one of the scientists who subscribe to the inland Bermuda Triangle theory.

"It is very possible that this, at one time, was a Bermuda Triangle water area which dried up. It may even have been linked directly to what we know today as the area encompassing the Triangle."

Together with colleague Dr. Hector Lopez-Loera, also a professor of geophysics at the university's Department of Geophysical Science, the scientists became deeply involved in trying to fathom the Zone's curious magnetic and radio anomalies.

Said Dr. Lopez-Loera: "The first things that attracted me were the highly unusual magnetic readings. It was very unusual to find so many reports of compasses and radios not working there.

"Our first study was magnetic, because of the problems

of the absorption of radio waves. In general, the area is almost normal, [with] a slightly higher background of magnetism, but not enough to be scientifically significant. But the further we probed, the more abnormalities we found.

"Out of every hundred readings, we would get one highly abnormal reading. So we did a large overall study to pinpoint the areas of abnormality.

"Oddly, we got jumps in reading less than ten inches apart. The normal magnetometer reading would be around five hundred for the whole area, but in selected areas of only five or ten meters wide, the readings would shoot up to two thousand and three thousand on the magnetometer.

"This machine measures the total composition of the magnetic field. What readings of this incredible magnitude mean is that there is some enormously magnetic body there, and there shouldn't be. We have never been able to find it.

"For example, San Ignacio Hill is made of basalt. This area is highly magnetic, though, and it shouldn't be. At the moment we have no reason why. We are just beginning to study this, and we don't know why the magnetic variances are so strong, or why there is such varied lack of range in radio transmissions.

"Another very abnormal thing is that we have found rocks which, as we understand, are not magnetic, but they also move the compass needle. This is very puzzling.

"We can only speculate right now. What we might have here, therefore, is a dryland Bermuda Triangle. It is on the exact same latitude as the Triangle."

Dr. Meritano has also studied the strange magnetic attraction of the basalt rocks found in the Zone, and only in the Zone.

"There are more basalts in this area than anywhere else in Mexico. And we find that here it is magnetic, but not elsewhere. I have never found material of the same magnetic property anywhere but in the Zone of Silence.

"We have no idea how this rock came to be here, or why it's here. In the last fifteen years, at least two large meteorites have fallen, and countless other smaller ones. We just do not understand why this area seems to attract meteorites.

"Compasses spin in the proximity of this magnetism, and radios don't work. But just two hundred to three hundred feet away, the compasses return to normal and the radios work. We have no idea how this rock came to be here, or why it is here. It is an enigma!"

Space Platforms

They rise out of the desert only a foot or so in height, but the area they cover is enormous. Nothing like them has been reported anywhere else in the world. Egypt has its pyramids, and the Zone of Silence has its curious giant platforms.

What they are, and why they should be there, is totally bewildering.

Nowhere in the recorded history of the landmass which constitutes Mexico is there any mention of the building of earthen platforms. As far as we know, no advanced culture has ever inhabited the Zone of Silence, so there is nothing to suggest that they might be prehistoric burial mounds—the most common explanation for unexplained useless humps of earth.

Yet they sit there defying reason.

The platforms are almost perfect rectangles, and many of them measure a staggering ten kilometers—or slightly over six miles—in length. They are almost indiscernible from ground level, but their vast size isn't appreciated until you attempt to follow their contours on foot. From the air it's a different story. The flat-topped mounds resemble gigantic runways or landing pads stretched to ridiculous lengths.

There is nothing unusual to report about the earth that has been used to build them; it's regular desert dirt which has been somehow compacted to form this peculiar kind of desert dais.

One very obvious fact about the platforms soon becomes apparent. Around the edges are unusual numbers of what appear to be meteorite fragments. Caution is used here to describe these strange rocks, because unlike regular meteorite debris, which contains a vast array of shapes and textures, the vast majority of the platform's fragments are perfectly smooth.

Why these black rocks should have taken on such a polished appearance is but another mystery. They might be of meteoritic origin, or they could even be natural rocks which have been "melted" into their present forms by some unknown forces.

Nobody has yet been able to supply one good line of logic to explain the giant raised platforms of the Zone. They are yet another unexplained curiosity which fits well with the UFOs and magnetism connection. Were they built as marker points for UFOs, exact landing spots where the richest sources of magnetism are ready and waiting to be tapped?

Today we have to build specially fortified landing strips for our massive heavy bombers, otherwise they'd churn into the earth like giant plows. Since the advent of the jumbo jets, commercial airport runways have had to be totally redesigned and engineered to accommodate the tremendous weight, landing speeds, and greatly increased stopping lengths. Despite the enormous new demands put on our airfields, nobody has yet designed an aircraft that needed a six-mile landing zone!

Were the Zone's platforms constructed to reinforce the desert floor for the phenomenal weights of intergalactic ships like the great Ceballo UFO? Are they remnants from when the Zone was a submerged seabed; underwater refueling pens for spacecraft, much like our present-day submarines?

Millions of Mysterious Meteorites

Littering the Zone of Silence are millions of meteorites. They take on fanciful shapes, glistening peardrops, baubles and beads, trinkets, possibly.

Pieces of ancient rock resemble brown glass bottles now become molten and splashed on the earth; burnished dollops spilled from unknown metal foundries. Polished ebony pebbles on a beach, some with spirals and curves, others just misshapen; a whole carnival of tiny geophysical freaks.

Pick one up to examine, and a smooth deep brown surface is discovered. A few are formed so perfectly smooth in the plunge from space that only a powerful magnifying glass reveals any pits in the surfaces.

In a strange way they are utterly beautiful natural works of art, and every one a unique original. They could be mounted and they'd probably sell like hotcakes in a Madison Avenue gallery, a pricey intergalactic version of the Pet Rock.

Scientists can only make a guess at where they came from, and how many, because the space radioactivity from meteorites which landed ages ago has long since bled into our earth and atmosphere. They can only form theories as to why they are so strangely attracted to the Zone of Silence, on a nightly basis.

And there is no question that the millions of meteorites

littering certain areas of the zones are "fresh." They sit on the surface of the baked desert floor.

The Zone's meteorites are surprisingly heavy, much heavier than regular terrestrial rocks or pebbles of the same size.

Every year the Zone experiences about a week of heavy rains, and the entire desert turns into a sea of mud. Those meteorites that had fallen in the previous months after the last rainy season would now sink down into the mud, disappearing forever from sight and forming yet another layer in the earth's crust.

The author was able to witness a typical meteorite field in the Zone and can attest to the fact that hundreds of thousands of meteorites were there to be picked up at random. And they were lying pristine and gleaming on the surface of the desert. They could have fallen the night before.

The total amount of meteorites to have plunged into the Zone is incalculable when it's considered that every year during the rainy season millions slip below the surface of the desert, only to be replaced by fresh falls.

If one wanted to corner the market on meteorites, it would be as easy as driving a truck into the Zone and literally loading up with tons of the extraterrestrial material. Millions of meteorites are there just for the taking.

And there is absolute proof that these strange objects basking in the desert sun are not of this planet.

Analysis of the Zone meteorites show that they are high in iron and nickel content—yet they display no attraction to magnetism. If these strange objects were of terrestrial origin they would have to show magnetic attraction because of their high metallic content.

Even though the Zone artifacts are mostly metal, they

defy the geophysical and magnetic laws for metals that have evolved on this planet. They have to be from outer space.

Proof of Ancient Astronauts?

The meteorites are positive links with space. But there also exist possible extraterrestrial artifacts in the Zone.

These are the rare metallic-rock combinations that have all the appearances of being hand- or machine-made by some form of intelligence.

Strange rocklike objects with straight metal grids and lines which run through them in perfect geometric patterns have been discovered in the Zone. Girderlike shapes, which give the appearance of metal spars from an unknown craft, rest twisted, tortured, fractured, and shattered on the desert floor.

This type of unexplained debris lies among the meteorites like the fossilized skeletal remains of long-extinct machines.

Are these strangely mechanical forms the legacy of prehistoric pilots who guided their UFO craft into the Zone, only to end in crash landings or to abandon them? Maybe they're the remains of a cosmic wrecking yard, all that's left after crippled UFO's have been butchered for their usable spare parts.

Around the Zone the inhabitants treasure these unique finds. To them there are only two solutions: They are leftovers from a superior civilization of ancestors, or they are the decayed remnants of the flying machines flown by ancient astronauts who once visited the Zone.

In scientific terms there are also two solutions: They're either terrestrial rocks and ores which have welded together in uniquely bizarre forms—or they're not!

How they came here then becomes a matter of conjecture.

One scientist to have viewed samples from the Zone is Dr. David Warburton, mineralogist and assistant professor of geology at Florida Atlantic University. He examined one of the strange alleged pieces from a UFO.

He admitted, "I have never seen rocks like this before. I never saw anything that looks remotely like this."

Closely examining the grid pattern on the sample, Dr. Warburton exclaimed, "The straight lines could be oxidized iron. There is a possibility that it is a piece of metal, a manufactured grid, which totally oxidized by being underwater for all those years, and then subsequently buried in the desert sands.

"The areas between the gridwork are filled with sandstone and silt. It could have been straight metal at one time, filled out with silt."

A puzzled Dr. Warburton added, "When you get strange magnetic readings in this area, it may indicate the impact of meteorites and iron from the sky. If this were a sample from a meteorite, I would expect it to be magnetic. It is not!"

The same catwalk-type grid sample was also studied at The Smithsonian Institution's Museum of Natural History in Washington, D.C., where it again created controversy.

Harold Banks, museum specialist in geology, could not pin down its origins, and he was equally mystified whether the sample was terrestrial or extraterrestrial. One test to prove it to be of natural Earth origin proved negative. The simple exercise to show a natural iron concentration is to scratch the rock on a hard piece of quartz. A terrestrial iron concentration will leave a brownish-reddish streak. When Banks attempted the test, no streak appeared.

"It should give me a streak on quartz, but it does not. Perhaps it has been exposed to fire at some time or another. There is iron in the veins of the object, which are very parallel."

The scientist admitted, "I have never seen anything quite like this—it is bizarre. It is one of the strangest rocks I have ever seen."

He agreed that the possibility existed that the strange sample was a piece of manufactured metal, with the grid openings possibly filling with sand during eons underwater, and then petrifying with time.

Another possibility was that the Zone rock was a subterranean nodule, formed in or on the seabed. "But subterranean nodules contain a central core, radiating outward, and we don't see that in this piece."

The examination continued. "I believe the base is an iron oxide concretion. This is not one solid rock. It is a layered sediment, and there is a great deal of geological time represented here. This piece may be well over sixty million years old."

If the sample from the Zone was that ancient, and indeed was not a natural geological formation, where did it come from?

Banks pointed out, "We don't know if this is the result of a mind of some sort which created it. We do know that sixty million years ago, no man had a metal forge making things on Earth. There is oxidized iron in these lines in the rock.

"Nobody was around manufacturing metal on Earth at that point, so, if it is a manufactured piece, it had to come from someplace else. If it is manufactured, it is not terrestrial—it could be something that crashed down there.

"Who knows, you could have an iron deposit, or a catwalk from an ancient UFO. That's the trouble with science, you can never answer all the possibilities. This is fascinating. I have never seen anything like it."

Parts of ancient UFOs, or just puzzling geological freaks? We may not know the true answer to these mysteries of the

Zone of Silence until scientific procedures can positively identify them—or our understanding of the universe, and the possibility of UFOs, and their occupants, being of extraterrestrial origin, becomes more complete.

Chapter 12

The Athena Mystery

"We're losing it! This damned rocket's got a mind of its own! . . ."

"I don't believe it. That's impossible—the fourth stage just ignited!"

"Is there any way we can get it down?"

"Sure, we can shoot the SOB out of the sky!"

"Oh, Christ, can't anybody do anything . . . it's heading for Mexico!"

THE PANIC IN the voices of the scientists at the missile guidance control center at Green River, Utah, was obvious enough. It was July 2, 1970, and an Athena rocket had suddenly gone renegade.

There had been over 150 successful firings since the Athena program was started in the early sixties. The predictability and great integrity of the Athena had made it a workhorse rocket, one that could be counted on for guidance, navigation, orbit, and reentry experiments. It was one spacecraft that was surefire and secure for testing just about everything from fruit to nuts in the space and military programs.

But on this very routine flight in the summer of 1970, something inexplicable happened. A rocket got away!

Revealed for the First Time

This amazing story has never been revealed before. It is being told here in detail for the first time.

With all the safety precautions built into military launches, a runaway Athena should have slammed back to earth in a "safe area" no more than thirty to forty miles off its expected trajectory. It didn't. Ignoring all commands, it streaked off on its own predestined course.

If everything had gone according to the plans of the missile experts and engineers, the rocket would have blasted its way through the stratosphere into near orbit; then it would have made a leisurely swoop through space to perform reentry tests as it broke back through the atmosphere for a landing at the White Sands Missile Range in New Mexico.

Instead, the wayward missile headed straight for Mexico . . . and the Zone of Silence.

In the early evening of July 2, some residents on the edge of the Zone saw an object plummeting to Earth. It was easily dismissed as of no consequence. One more unexplained falling light is nothing new to this part of the world where meteorites shower like rain and curious UFO lights buzz the desert constantly.

Rosendo Aguilera was probably nearer than anybody to where the rocket landed. Don Rosendo recalled: "I was working on a water tank on my ranch. I heard a muffled explosion, more like a thud, as if something had hit the desert.

"I looked up in the direction from where it came, but I could see nothing. It seemed to me that the noise came from the direction of San Ignacio Hill, probably about five kilometers away. I paid no more attention to it."

Don Rosendo's observations were to prove to be crucial later in the game, and the "Athena Incident" was to become a major embarrassment for the U.S. military, and an international wrangle for the Mexican authorities.

Exactly why it made this bizarre course change to land in the heart of the Zone is still a total mystery. What had drawn it from its normal course to head toward a remote spot almost nine hundred miles downrange and some four hundred miles farther than its target? How come it didn't drop to Earth when radio instructions had already directed its powerful engines to quit? Why had one stage of the rocket fired up without command to unexplainably steer it directly into the Zone?

The hurried, official hard-line explanation was some sort of "mechanical or navigational" failure. But rumors buzzed Green River that the rocket had been diverted by a force that nobody was able to account for.

The shocking impact of the idea that something, or somebody, had been able to "hijack" a U.S. military rocket resulted in an immediate stone wall of secrecy.

Blackout

Within twenty-four hours a complete blackout was imposed on news releases as frustrated scientists scratched their heads and tried first to figure out not just how their missile had been abducted—but to where exactly!

It was to be four weeks before the nose cone was

recovered, and to this day an official version of the incident is yet to be released.

The space scientists involved have been unable to come up with a solution to the Athena mystery. It became an even more acute embarrassment for the U.S. military when they could give no logical explanation to Mexico for the errant flight which had, after all, crash-landed in another government's country.

Because of the hush-hush nature of the incident, the entire Athena program was put on the back burner for seven months and questions were raised right up to Pentagon and White House levels.

But in piecing together the Athena mystery some things become very clear:

• The missile had begun to stray wildly off course when the ground technicians decided to "pull the plug" on the mission.
• Without power the reentry vehicle should have crash-landed within an unpopulated wilderness of Utah.
• The third- and fourth-stage rockets were intact, but "dead," at the time of mission abort.
• No technician sent any electronic command to ignite the remaining engines. Radio-wave monitoring showed absolutely no spurious signals in the area.
• Incredibly, the fourth stage received a command to ignite for approximately five seconds.
• The five-second burn sent it directly into the Zone of Silence.
• U.S. scientists were so disoriented by the freak episode that it took them weeks to actually pinpoint the exact crash site.

Colonel Thomas C. Kearns, director of facility engineering at White Sands during the shot, admitted the incident was played down. "It was a little mistake. We don't really advertise our failures. There wasn't any wide publicity about it. To be honest, we don't know what threw it off course."

The missile expert describes the Athena as one of the safest and most successful spacecraft ever developed. It was utilized, mainly by the Air Force, as a high-altitude test rocket for carrying research payloads. Kearns is careful to point out that the rocket was not being utilized as a weapons system, although it did carry a radioactive payload, cobalt 57.

This fact alone was to spark off an international incident between the U.S. military and Mexican authorities who viewed the radioactive levels with lethal suspicion.

The Athena's cargo of cobalt had been loaded into the nose cone of the rocket for an experiment to test the effects of reentry on the exterior surface of the rocket's nose. The cobalt was utilized in a highly sensitive instrumentation center.

Missile specialist Leonard Sugerman, one of the top men on the project and assistant to the director of the Physical Science Laboratory at the State University of New Mexico in Las Cruces, explained the "innocence" of the radioactive cobalt's role.

"This particular flight was an ablations test, measuring the removal of nose-cone material, by melting or vaporization, as it plunges back through the atmosphere. The whole purpose is to see what happens to the nose cone. You can measure how fast things are burning away by putting radioactive material in the nose cone and attaching it to sensors. As exterior material wears away, the readings on radioactive meters get stronger and stronger as the skin of the nose cone sloughs away during reentry."

Even today, experts like Sugerman are nonplussed by

the Athena's strange behavior. Sugerman, a retired Air Force colonel, was test conductor for the ill-fated Athena.

"I remember the shot vividly," recalls Sugerman. "The reentry vehicle malfunctioned and it landed about four hundred miles south of the border. I don't think anyone has been able to pin down what exactly happened to cause it. It was a combination of things that seemed impossible.

"It's like the Bermuda Triangle—the thing just got away from us! It was something that should never have happened. It should have come down and broken up. It could have gone into orbit, it could have burned up, it could have easily hit Mexico City, it could have gone anywhere in the world. Why did it decide to fly into this particular area? Nobody knows. It's still a puzzle.

"I can tell you one thing. We breathed one giant sigh of relief when we found out it had hit a spot even more desolate than the White Sands range itself."

Strange Odyssey

The Athena is a four-stage rocket, with the first two engines firing up to blast it some two hundred miles above the earth's surface. The third- and fourth-stage engines were used to bring it into reentry position and propel it back to Earth.

On its launchpad the rocket stands fifty-four feet high and weighs seven tons. In flight it could reach speeds in excess of four thousand miles per hour, and its brief trip from Green River to White Sands should have taken approximately eight minutes.

Sugerman put together the story of the strange flight of the deranged rocket.

"Once it's up there, going straight up, the part that would bring it back down, the reentry vehicle, would pitch over and when it hit the right angle the third and fourth stages would be fired to bring it home. This would really slam the thing back down into the atmosphere. If the missile did not pitch over at the correct angle, the specialists on the ground would leave it; they'd do nothing to it and it would just drop out of the sky.

"Without power it would twist and tumble through the atmosphere, probably breaking up, and fall back into a national park in Utah, known as a safety dropout area. This had happened before. From a range safety point of view, if it didn't pitch over and assume the correct reentry angle we let it fall to the ground. They never went very far, probably thirty or forty miles off course.

"We know this didn't happen on this particular shot. It didn't turn over to reenter, and the ground control decided to let it drop. While it was still pointing upward, for some unknown reason the fourth stage ignited, and this kicked off the reentry vehicle on its way to Mexico.

"The big question here is not only why the fourth stage fired, but how it was able to ignite before the third stage. Something had to signal the fourth stage to fire, we know it must have received a signal to fire, that's the only possible explanation. But where it came from is still a mystery. Strange things happen, maybe a freak signal from a police vehicle on the ground, or a radio system in Albuquerque. Nobody knows where the signal came from.

"Experts tried to backtrack during the investigation, and they came up with all possible combinations of things. But one thing they did know for certain was that no ground signal was ever sent from Green River. Frequencies are monitored, so we know that there's nothing on the wavelength, no spurious signals, to affect the missile.

"They studied it for months before they came up with an accident report which said this happened; the fourth stage definitely received word to kick off. Maybe it came from Mexico, maybe it came from outer space. I don't think we'll ever find out for sure.''

Witch-Hunt

An internal witch-hunt was launched. As a result, the Athena program was put on hold for at least seven months while the knotty problem of recovering the nose cone from a neighboring country was worked out. And questions all the way up to the presidential level had to be answered.

Near the Zone itself, people like Police Chief Chaparro and Mayor Silva had been alerted by the local government that a suspected runaway rocket had homed in on their area.

"Sure, we told them it's in the Zone. Of course, where else would it go?" says a laconic Chaparro, with a smile.

But the truth at the time was that nobody knew exactly where the radioactive nose cone was—least of all the boffins from Green River and White Sands. They traced their trajectory plans, calculated fuel deployment, had rough radar fixes, and played with large clear perspex board maps and grease pencils, and still all they knew was that their wayward baby was somewhere over the border.

The American embassy in Mexico City was informed, and in a matter of hours the official telephone lines burned with a frenzy of calls between the U.S. and Mexico—most of them very apologetic. There's a big difference between "Sir, can we have our ball back?" and "Excuse me, senor, but would you mind returning our only slightly radioactive missile?"

There is no doubt that high-level panic set in when Mexican officials discovered that the missile "warhead" had been carrying radioactive cobalt. After all, it could have landed on Mexico City. First the Mexicans had to be reassured that no warhead was on the missile. This took some doing, because the suspicious government needed a very convincing reason why radioactive material should be in any peacetime nose cone to start with.

Then there was the sticky problem of trying to explain to the nervous Mexicans that nobody knew exactly where the rocket had landed.

In a lighthearted moment, it's said (probably apocryphally), a senior Mexican official quipped to a ranking U.S. military officer in New York, "Why don't you guys try our famous Zone of Silence? All the garbage from space gets dumped there!"

Frenzied Search

The first pioneering recovery teams from the U.S. rolled into Ceballos two days later.

Local guides were immediately recruited by U.S. Colonel Lowell R. Kuizle. Colonel Thomas Kearns traveled from White Sands to join the hunt. Guides were necessary to direct them through the uncharted areas of the Zone.

The Mexican military sent Major Julian Salas, Captain Jaime Gonzalez Sepulveda, and Colonel Vazquez Barete to join forces with the searchers from the U.S. Also accompanying them was Dr. Enrique Bravo from the Mexican National Nuclear Energy Commission.

Teams of local workers were put on the military payroll to form a horseback posse to scour the wastelands for the bandit from the sky.

One of the U.S. recovery team members was Sergio Plaza, an installations engineer from White Sands.

"I had heard of the Zone of Silence. It was a fantastic experience to actually go down there," recalls Plaza.

Plaza acted as civil engineer and official interpreter for the expedition. Also crowding into tiny Ceballos, together with the military officers and civilian technicians, were members from the U.S. Atomic Energy Commission—a fact that the Mexican authorities didn't take lightly—and representatives from Mexico City.

"The local people, they thought the missile had been attracted by that area somehow," says Plaza. "Of course, we didn't believe that; we didn't admit to it, anyway. It just went out of control. It was our own booboo, a U.S. mistake, so there wasn't any publicity at the time.

"It should have headed for the White Sands missile base, but it went to Ceballos. Nobody knows for sure whether a magnetic pull from this area caused the missile to go off course. That area is pretty powerful; they have meterorite showers down there every night, you know. . . ."

After days of fruitless searching there wasn't a sniff of the elusive Athena. In desperation, search parties were then lined up shoulder to shoulder to attack the vast wilderness.

It came as a surprise to the now-weary Mexican searchers that the gringo military hadn't brought more sophisticated tracking equipment with them. A few light planes were spotted above Ceballos and flying low over the surrounding desert, but they had returned empty-handed. American military pilot George Koppmann had been scouring the desert for days without any luck.

Recalled Major Silva, "We thought that maybe they didn't want to frighten people. You know, with all the talk about radioactivity. I got the feeling they just wanted to get this thing quietly and get out."

But things didn't go quite according to plan.

Admits Colonel Kearns, "We were nonplussed. We knew it had to be out there somewhere."

The Mexicans' Captain Jaime Sepulveda got the first lucky break when word reached him that Don Rosendo had heard or seen something land in the desert near San Ignacio

Hill on July 2. Piecing the sketchy details together, he calculated that the rocket might be somewhere in a region of five to ten kilometers around the hill.

This possible site gained even more credibility when other Mexican troops reported back that Antonio Munoz, a resident of the tiny village of Glorias de Quintero on the edge of the Zone, had reported seeing an object fall near San Ignacio Hill.

U.S. military officials then decided to call in further help. A private company from Las Vegas was hired to provide a specially equipped plane to sweep the Zone. On board was a scintillation counter, a device which detects and measures radioactivity.

Flown by civilian pilots Edward Shultz and John Kleland, Beechcraft B50 N 702-B swooped over the suspected area of the desert combing meridians 103 to 106 west on the 26th parallel near San Ignacio Hill.

And then, bingo!

Kleland, monitoring the scintillator, suddenly picked up a higher reading than the normal background radiation.

"This has gotta be it!" Kleland cried out. "Bank her around and let's run over it again."

Sure enough, on a second, closer pass over a small mesa some fifty or so feet below them, the counter on the machine went haywire.

"There she is. That's cobalt, no doubt about it." The jubilant Kleland whistled.

And, in one of the most unceremonious marking ceremonies ever, they tossed out bags of flour onto the small outcrop to identify it for the searchers on the ground; simple, but effective.

For Colonel Kearns and the other searchers, the Zone had played one of its bizarre tricks. Out of all the hundreds of square miles of boringly flat desert, the Athena had landed on top of a mesa, just high enough to hide it from the view of searchers on horseback or foot.

Radiation

The first search crew to reach the crash site approached with extreme caution. Nobody knew exactly how much of the potentially deadly radiation had spilled out of the nose cone.

Like sci-fi robots, two radiation experts armed with Geiger counters probed forward. Clad in full-length metallic suits with clear plastic face visors, they were sweltering under the intense desert sun as their heavy white boots edged toward the mesa and up its steep sides. Although the radiation readings were higher than normal, the experts in the strange suits deduced that there was no danger to human life.

The intense month-long search ended on top of the mesa on August 3. The site was 1,150 feet above sea level.

Colonel Kearns stared down into a crater and breathed a sigh of relief. But what he saw did nothing to make him happy. The Athena was almost completely obliterated, and that also went for its cargo of cobalt 57.

It had created a crater fifty feet long, sixteen feet wide, and ten feet deep. The spot was eight kilometers north of San Ignacio Hill. The exact crash site was logged as meridian 103 degrees 45 minutes west at parallel 26 degrees 45 minutes north.

The impact had completely destroyed the rocket; only tangled metal and fragments of the equipment it carried aboard remained in the hole in the desert.

Recalled engineer Plaza, "We found the capsule at the bottom of the crater. There wasn't much left of it, just scraps of metal and stuff."

Whatever clues to the wayward rocket's disappearing

act the scientists might have hoped to discover, they now looked very slim indeed.

Their primary concern was now with the effects of the radiation spill. Readings showed increased radiation within an area of approximately a mile around the crater. As a safety precaution to protect the animal wildlife, every single bush and cactus within this zone was put to the torch.

Colonel Kearns plays down the radiation aspect.

"There was a radioactive payload, not enough to be serious but enough to be technically radioactive," he confirms. "We had long negotiations with the State Department and the Mexican government about bringing it back and neutralizing the area.

"My job was to evacuate whatever had to be taken out. There was a certain roentgen reading [the international unit for measuring radioactivity], but it was not all that radioactive. The whole area reduced to a background of about .1, which meant we weren't dealing with very much."

But if the American military men once believed they could just walk out of the Zone with what was left of their rocket, they had another thought coming.

A Railroad to Nowhere

The Mexican government began to play hardball over the radiation issue. And now the engineers found themselves having to dismantle the desert.

"The Mexican authorities said the radiation was too high, so they told us to remove all the contaminated dirt and take it back with us to the States. By our standards at White Sands, the background radiation was nothing. It was well within limits. We had rockets bouncing in there all the time with radiation levels like this. It was quite normal. The Mexicans didn't see it that way; it was supposedly too high for their standards,'' admits Kearns.

''We brought a few drums of dirt back that were of a certain roentgen reading.''

According to the recollections of the folk in and around Ceballos, those ''few drums'' turned out to be the whole mesa and most of the surrounding desert.

And the U.S. military went to the expense and time of building an entire railroad line into the Zone to remove the debris. The spur ran from near the crash site to join the main line at Carrillo station some fifteen miles away.

''We had to remove the dirt. Yes, it did go by train,'' was all that engineer Plaza said he was able to confirm.

Even more amazing, the American engineers constructed an entire airstrip in the desert, capable of accommodating medium and heavy cargo planes. This, above anything, caused the most resentment from the local population. The people of normally sleepy Ceballos complained bitterly about the noise of the aerial invasion lumbering in and out of the Zone twenty-four hours a day.

What exactly necessitated the influx of so many aircraft was never quite explained, but dozens of heavy-duty bulldozers and trucks were soon rumbling around the desert floor, strange yellow-painted juggernauts creating a permanent smoke screen of dust around the site.

American security officials dictated that the spot on top of the mesa be sealed from prying eyes. A high wall of canvas was constructed around the site, and residents in the area were warned to keep clear. Most of the Mexican labor was dismissed and told never to return.

Laboring frantically, the recovery team worked in shifts, two hours on and two hours off, to avoid the deadly effects of the sun's baking heat. They were also fortified with rations of vitamins flown in specially from the U.S. The fading brown packages containing B and C vitamins were marked with the date 1945.

Steel boxes were constantly being carried between the mesa and the airstrip. These reinforced and insulated caskets carried the last remnants of the wayward rocket.

Although the main body of the wreckage was atop the mesa, the engineers were amazed to discover that fragments were being found up to a quarter of a mile around the crater. This was disturbing because it suggested an explosion on impact, a violent ending that might have spread the radiation even farther than at first expected.

Today, bits of wire, fragments of electronic wiring boards, and torn and twisted bits of metal are still being found in the desert nearby. Some of these remaining artifacts— without any detectable radiation—are now on display in an exhibition at the Federal Palace in Torreon.

Mayor Silva insists that the entire cleanup operation went on for months. "Thousands of barrels, maybe millions, nobody ever kept count. They hauled them away in railroad cars.

"Then there were the other things they took back, the rocks, the meteorites, and my animals. It was good business for us while it lasted.

"You realize, you have much of the Zone in the U.S. now. I don't know where, though."

There is no doubt that the American military men transported many samples of the Zone's strange wildlife back to the U.S. for further study. Witnesses confirm that parties were sent out to collect plants, insects, rodents, and reptiles, including the giant land tortoises and the huge centipedes of the Zone.

But one thing is certain—the desert was many hundreds of tons lighter when the Americans finally departed.

The Official View

The official book on the Athena incident has been closed by the Pentagon. It's not a subject that anybody wants to readily discuss. Nobody took the responsibility, nobody took any blame.

Dr. Luis Maeda, who has chronicled much of what went on during the Athena incident from the Mexican viewpoint, admits, "Any questions raised by the Athena incident have been met with complete and absolute silence. Government documents relating to the incident have been sealed both in the U.S. and Mexico."

Dr. Maeda, one of the Zone's most knowledgeable and persistent researchers, asks the following questions:

"Why did the Athena rocket fly more than eight hundred kilometers from its original planned landing site? Is it really the magnetic attraction in this area that caused it to come down? Could there be a magnetic vortex or cone that reaches up like a Van Allen window to assist the falling of objects from space in this area?"

And Dr. Maeda adds, "Don't forget that only the previous year the Zone attracted a thirteen-thousand-million-year-old meteorite from space, the most famous meteorite to land on the planet."

For some still unfathomable reason a tried and tested missile, equipped with the latest in ballistics technology and a sophisticated guidance system, strayed from its path and zoomed straight for the Zone. Of that there is no doubt.

It still seems curious that a fourth-stage engine would receive a mysterious signal to power it with pinpoint accuracy directly into the Zone of Silence. How this could have happened to such sophisticated technology has never been answered. It was the same advanced American high technology that had put men on the moon, and brought them home, just the previous year!

The Mexican government, however, washed its hands of the affair as soon as the last drumload from the Zone of Silence left bound for the U.S. . . . from the railroad spur with no name.

Chapter 13

Conclusions and Theories

OF ALL THE explanations and theories about the Zone of Silence, nothing is quite as enticing as linking it to the mysterious Bermuda Triangle as an inland twin.

During the final preparation of this manuscript, the author had a long discussion with Charles Berlitz, considered by most respected researchers of the paranormal as the "father" of investigations into the infamous Triangle. Berlitz's best-selling books *The Bermuda Triangle* and *Without Trace* have become the definitive bibles for those fascinated by the enigmatic stretch of ocean where people and craft disappear, swallowed up into unseen voids to vanish forever.

Although there have been no confirmed reports of people vanishing without trace in the Zone, the simple explanation for this might be that the area is so desolate and its climate so unforgiving that few would ever want to venture there, and would certainly do so at their own peril. Private pilots prefer not to fly over or around the Zone because of the instrument anomalies it causes, although there are no official directives from the Mexican-government version of the Federal Aviation Administration. But the author has received confirmation on a number of occasions from numerous senior sources within commercial U.S. and Mexican airlines, including pilots themselves, of this one fact: It is an unwritten law that no flights are ever scheduled to cross the air mass above the Zone.

Berlitz is the first to confirm that the similarities in anomalies between the Zone and the Triangle are so striking that they just cannot be ignored as possible paranormal twins. The respected investigator and chronicler of the Triangle admitted, "I have long been fascinated with the mysteries of la Zona del Silencio."

He continued: "It is one of the most mysterious spots on the planet, and one that I have always wanted to investigate personally. Unlike the Triangle it is a rich subject for intensive scientific research because of its accessibility and the repeatable nature of the phenomena occurring there. We may well learn much from la Zona that may hold keys to solve riddles from the Triangle."

Future science, no doubt, will provide answers to many of the intriguing issues presented by the Zone, but without serious scientific funding this may be years away. The Mexican government, together with UNESCO, is blazing a scientific trail with the Biospheric Laboratory at the heart of the Zone, and this single multimillion-dollar venture has provided a well-needed spur to promote enthusiasm from the traditional scientific establishment. Pemex, the government-owned and -run Mexican petroleum industry, is also pouring millions of pesos into subterranean research around the area of the Zone in the belief that its unique geophysical qualities may well provide a natural harbor for vast untapped oceans of oil, gas, and mineral wealth.

The mysteries of the Zone may well transcend science as we know it, venturing into different dimensions and providing previously unknown insights into the cosmos beyond our world, so it is from both the scientific and philosophical perspectives that we will endeavor to provide some clues to a rationale for some of the bizarre oddities taking place within the Zone.

As was stated at the beginning of this book, probing just one single anomaly from the Zone of Silence, and coming up with theories or explanations, inevitably raises even more profound questions. It would be all too easy to promote wild speculation about the Zone, its bizarre animals, plantlife mutations, and UFOs. The possibilities of visits from ancient astronauts, lost civilizations, and even a race of primitive people or yetilike monsters are all theories that have been proposed and discussed in appropriate parts of this book.

But this chapter will take a unique approach and look at the Zone through the eyes of a hard-nosed scientist. This does not mean that the following views contain all the right answers; much has to be theory and conjecture, and when one deals with the Zone of Silence, the power of the unknown and of dimensions unseen cannot be discounted.

An Interview with Dr. Sergio Flores

Dr. Sergio Enrique Flores y Nava has one of Mexico's most brilliant and original minds. He is an expert in the chemical sciences and a postdoctoral graduate of Stanford University.

Dr. Flores's unique talents in organic chemistry have taken him to research professorships at the University of Warwick in England, the University of Paris, and universities in Brazil, Chile, Peru, and Venezuela. His special expertise in mass spectroscopy led to senior scientific positions with multinational chemical concerns like the giant DuPont corporation.

Among his specialties is the determination of the chemical structures of hormones, and Dr. Flores was one of the elite scientists at Syntex laboratories who developed the world's first human birth control pill.

Dr. Flores is also a rebel. At age fifty-seven, with jet-black hair and a small Zapata mustache, he could be taken for a man twenty years younger. A Mexican by birth, he is far from the orthodox academic image. His latest wife and devoted coresearcher, Mia, is a striking, lithesome California blonde who's young enough to easily be his daughter. Dr. Flores is a father many times over, and by his own account has had at least eight natural children that he knows of during his years of scientific globe-trotting. His lightning-fast brain, futuristic thinking, and untraditional views have often made him controversial in the eyes of the more austere established scientific hierarchy, despite his wealth of scientific expertise and industrial accolades.

And maybe this is why this swashbuckling scientific renegade has recently turned detective and avid investigator of the Zone of Silence.

After numerous field expeditions to the Zone, Dr. Flores has amassed a wealth of scientific information, facts, and fiction on the mysterious area. He is now in the process of compiling the first scientifically objective cataloging of Zone phenomena. Through his scientific enthusiasm, and not-too-insignificant powers of persuasion, Dr. Flores has also sparked an increasing interest among other researchers from many diverse scientific disciplines to investigate the Zone.

It is because of Dr. Flores's background and his devotion to all matters pertaining to the Zone that he was a natural choice to provide a unique brand of insight into this strangest of spots on our planet.

Following are highlights of an interview with Dr. Flores, granted exclusively for this book.

AUTHOR: Dr. Flores, people outside Mexico have heard little about the Zone of Silence. Why do you think this is so?

FLORES: We Mexicans traditionally are very closemouthed about things we are unable to account for or explain. The Zone of Silence is a very mysterious place. Previously it might have been considered scientific suicide among one's peers to support the existence of the anomalies within the Zone. But now a growing number of scientists are accepting the fact that strange unexplained phenomena do take place in the Zone, and, to be honest, it's becoming quite acceptable and almost the "in thing" to investigate the Zone. At one time the local government would deny the existence of such a place, but today the Ministry of Tourism especially is recognizing that tremendous interest in the Zone.

A: Do you believe there is a connection between the Zone and the Bermuda Triangle?

F: At first glance it looks quite ridiculous. But when one looks at the geophysical formation of the zone and considers it was once part of a thriving living ancient ocean, then the link begins to sound much stronger. Both the Zone and the Triangle are on the 27th parallel only a few hundred miles apart, and before the shifts of the continents and the movements of the underground jigsaw puzzle, the tectonic plates that form the surface of the earth's crust, it is entirely possible that eons ago the Zone and the Triangle were part of one and the same sea. It's therefore easy to accept that what phenomena are taking place in the Triangle could easily be being duplicated inland in the Zone.

A: Much has been made of the strange magnetic anomalies in the zone. What do you make of them? Is there a geophysical answer?

F: I believe there are geophysical explanations, possibly

more than one. But I must stress that these are theories, speculation only. Deep under the Zone there could exist great deposits of shifting plasma. These plasmas could be vast oceans of water, oil, or magma. It is known that when huge subterranean fluid plasma deposits exist, the result can be an effect on normal terrestrial magnetism. They can interfere with the existing magnetism to produce magnetic vortexes. It can be likened to a whirlpool effect, a similar type of phenomenon that we witness with tornados and twisters which disrupt the normal currents of airflow. In the case of the Zone, the moving plasmas, if they are large enough, can distort the existing magnetic pull between the poles. They may even produce localized phenomena, where magnetic eddies or whirlpools exert a local effect on the magnetic field.

A: Would this affect radio waves and communications?

F: Oh, yes, this is entirely possible. The magnetic vortexes can reflect, block, or distort radio waves. Because of the localized incidences of magnetic changes, we believe this is why radio signals can get through in some spots, and only yards away they may be completely absent, blocked or diverted through a pool of magnetism.

A: How would you explain the magnetic rocks found within the Zone? We have witnessed experiments where even small rocks will dramatically change compass readings, dragging the needle away from true magnetic north or pushing it in an opposite direction. When the rocks are rotated, the compass needles take on different positions, sometimes not even following the rotation of the rock.

F: There are many of these rocks to be found in the Zone, some small, some huge. These are definitely rocks with no ore content, and rocks should not be magnetic. It is the only place in the world where I have witnessed this phenomenon. It is my belief that the rocks were originally from a vast pool of magma beneath the earth's crust, the same magma that could display these curious magnetic anomalies we just talked about. As the magma broke through to the surface and cooled to form solid rock, so it therefore retained the individual magnetic shifts, or variations, found in its "parent" plasma pool. The polarity would be different.

A: Do you believe in the theory that a giant meteorite might have crashed into the Zone during ancient times and be embedded deep in the earth? If the meteorite was substantial enough and had a high ferrous content, could this produce strange shifts in magnetism?

F: It's an interesting theory, but one that I would find hard to prove. Certainly we do know that meteorites shower down on the Zone in quantities unknown elsewhere on the earth. The Allende meteorite, one of the greatest the modern world has seen, was drawn to the zone. An enormous deposit of iron ore could have the effect of "bending" the magnet field. It is also known that radio transmissions have to be boosted to almost unheard-of levels to get them over large ore mines.

A: So wouldn't this giant-meteorite theory make more sense to explain the magnetic and radio-wave anomalies?

F: Well, I have one major problem with it. There are literally millions of meteorites to be found scattered around the desert floor in the Zone. We have examined them and are presently performing much more sophisticated spectroscopic analysis. One thing is for sure: These meteorites are made up of something like 90 percent of iron—but it is nonmagnetic. The ferrous material contained in these meteorites will not attract a magnet. This is why we can be so positive that the meteorites we find in the Zone are not terrestrial geophysical artifacts. They have to be extraterrestrial because all iron on and in the earth exhibits proper-

ties of magnetic attraction, and these meteorites definitely
do not.

A: Let's stay with the meteorites for a moment. Having
myself witnessed the vast meteorite fields within the Zone,
and having collected dozens of them, I know that they
come in some pretty bizarre sizes and shapes. Is this usual
for meteorites?

F: It's really fascinating. But because we do not see
meteorites showering down on earth every day as they do in
the Zone, and meteorite samples are extremely rare and
very hard to come by, we really don't know what is
ordinary and what isn't. Certainly the meteorites of the
Zone come in every shape and form imaginable. No two
that I have found have had identical shapes. Some look
like peardrops, some are like balls, others even look like
pipes or cylinders, or like drops of molten metal. The
infinite variety of meteorite sizes and shapes in the Zone
taunts the imagination. The shapes alone are very mysterious. Because we know that they are composed of 90
percent iron and they are not attracted to magnetism, they
must have a very peculiar atomic structure. Man-made
stainless steel may have a similar atomic structure because
it too is not subject to normal magnetic attraction. It is
known that if you take a metallic structure, say the fuselage of a 747 jet, and subject it to intense radiation, you
can observe changes in the atomic structures of the metals;
metals like aluminum can degrade to irons. This is a
proven fact. I have a very strange theory, and this is highly
speculative, that we may not be looking at traditional
meteorites as we imagine them: as natural parts of the
cosmos that were formed in the Big Bang and have traversed
time and space to end up on the earth. What we might be
observing, however, are the remains of some giant metallic craft or object which disintegrated in the farthest reaches

of space and its remnants are now showering onto the earth.

A: Do you mean a UFO?

F: Well, I wouldn't like to put a name to it. But use your own imagination.

A: Do the shapes of the meteorites give you any clues to the possibility of their being UFO artifacts?

F: I don't think I'd like to be drawn on this. Certainly the strangeness of shape of some meteorites can lead one to imagine them as small portions of pipes or conduits. Some samples even appear to be hollow inside. I have heard of meteorite samples forming grid patterns, as if they were following some sort of logical formation. But I have never found any of them myself. The meteorite shapes are a mystery, very mysterious.

A: Why do you think meteorites are so strangely attracted to the Zone and not other areas of the world?

F: Some have theorized that it could be the intense magnetism of the Zone, but there again we know that the extraterrestrial objects we find are not subject to magnetic pull. That's another mystery.

A: Do you have any rationale?

F: I subscribe to the theory that the Zone acts like a cosmic window to the universe.

A: Is this what other scientists have referred to as a similar effect to Van Allen windows?

F: Yes, exactly. This is known physics. High up in the atmosphere there are rings, possibly of magnetic origin, which shield the earth from cosmic radiation; they act as filters. But in certain spots there are holes or gaps in these protective layers. You can call them windows. The Van Allen windows are well documented; in fact, NASA has them mapped out. And what is rather strange is that the majority of them appear on the 27th parallels both above and below the equator, 27th parallel north and 27th parallel south.

A: Is there a Van Allen window above the Zone?

F: We believe so, and this may account for cosmic debris being drawn through this window into the Zone.

A: How does this affect the Zone as far as radiation goes?

F: This is an important point that we are actively investigating at the moment, and it may lead to many answers for the strange phenomena of the Zone. When you get a hole in the protective belt of the upper atmosphere, it can allow all sorts of known and unknown radiation to beam down. This, in essence, is really known and unknown energy. The entire region of the Zone, and possibly the Bermuda Triangle, could be bathed in unknown energies.

A: Can these energies affect things like compasses and gyros?

F: Absolutely. In fact, as far back as 1964, during the early U.S. space program, General Electric put out a technical information guide explaining how unfiltered cosmic radiation, energies that we normally do not observe on the earth, can affect missiles, radio systems, and satellites. This is very important for navigation and the functioning of electrical systems.

A: So the Zone may be getting unnatural forces from two directions?

F: Yes, exactly. From cosmic radiation and the magnetic anomalies we know to exist at the terrestrial level. That is the simple reason why airline pilots prefer not to fly over the Zone. Sensitive instruments can behave bizarrely when bombarded by strange energies, especially when they are coming from two directions, from above and below.

A: What about the strange plant and animal life, the purple cacti, the unusual tortoises, albino snakes, et cetera, et cetera?

F: We believe the excesses of cosmic radiation may play a significant role here as well. Let's take the cacti first. The initial thing we are trying to do with the red and purple cacti is to get them recognized in an official botanical classification. Nothing like them exists in the botanical literature. For this we are enlisting the services of Dr. Helia Bravo Unam. She is one of the foremost botanists in our country. We feel that the purple cacti and cactus trees have a separate genetic makeup from the regular green cacti. What has caused this we do not know. It could be the effects of cosmic radiation. But most certainly we do not believe the unnatural colors are a result of chemical deposits in the desert earth. They would have to be very localized and extremely specific to cause one cactus to grow purple and the one next to it green. But there is another side to the coin, possibly one that may relate to a more natural biochemical explanation. The green color we experience in all plantlife comes from the chlorophyll, and chlorophyll molecules have a nucleus containing magnesium. It is possible that in the skin of the purple cacti the nucleus of magnesium has been replaced by one of iron. It is iron that gives our blood cells their red color.

A: So what about the animals?

F: Again, we believe that cosmic radiation may be responsible. It is known that the neutrons from some types of radiation can result in increased alpha particles, and these are known to affect living cells. Atomic radiation results in alpha particles, and these can cause changes in the genetic codes of living cells, producing positive and negative mutations. An example of negative mutation might be the proliferation of cancer cells. An example of a positive mutation might be a color, or surface mutation, that might protect against further mutant effects of increased radiation. The purple cacti may display this effect, and the yellow rings in the eyes of the Zone tortoises may be a protective mutation. Albino animals are known to spring from genetic mutations, and this may apply to the snakes and lizards of the area.

A: But what about the lack of a tail among the Zone tortoises? Zoologists claim the tail is essential for the mating process.

F: Well, a tail may be essential for every other species of tortoise, but the giant tortoises of the Zone seem to be doing very well without it. The species is thriving. Of course, there is another way we can look at the land tortoises of the Zone, and that is from an evolutionary perspective. The Zone was once an ocean, and the tortoises that exist there today as a clearly distinct species may have evolved from giant sea turtles. The evolutionary process would have adapted them to land as the great sea began to dry up, and it is highly likely that they evolved with qualities more like the swimming and mating habits of the sea turtles than the true native land tortoises seen elsewhere in Mexico.

A: UFOs . . . they seem to abound in the zone. Do you have any theories about UFO sightings and the strange lights that dance around the Zone?

F: The lights may have a sound scientific explanation, although this does not answer their reported peculiarity of propulsion or movement. In an article published in the scientific magazine *Nature* many years ago, a British physicist claimed to have the answer to something that sounds very similar to the phenomenon of lights in the Zone, and this was attributed to a strange magnetic force field. In 1811 the scientist, a Dr. A. J. Blair from Devon, claimed to have witnessed a startling phenomenon in the bell tower of a small church in the village of Stamford-Courtney. The bells were being rung, and as it happened a particularly violent thunderstorm was raging outside. Suddenly the bells froze in midair; they were stopped dead suspended in midswing. Dr. Blair reported that it was as if the bells, which weighed many tons, were being held apart by some giant unseen hand. He deduced that the bells had been trapped, frozen in an immense magnetic force field produced by the oscillations of electricity produced by the thunderstorm activity. The bells were seen to glow, and apparently fireballs danced around them. The bells were held frozen in space for a number of seconds before being released from the strange magnetic hold. We know that in the Zone there are strange magnetic anomalies, and we know that unusual cosmic energies and possibly unknown sources of electrical stimulation may occur. When we combine all these factors together, it could possibly produce a form of supermagnetism and what appear to be lights or fireballs.

A: What about the great Ceballos UFO, and the floating city witnessed by Don Rosendo and his peons?

F: I have no wish to doubt the integrity of the people of Ceballos. They are honest and God-fearing people. I do believe they saw something that they could not account for, something truly unexplainable, and possibly something that our present scientific knowledge has no explanation for. UFOs are a respected scientific phenomenon these days, although we have developed no scientific logic for them. I firmly believe they saw a UFO, but whatever giant unidentified flying object it was, I do not know.

A: And Don Rosendo's floating city?

F: I have puzzled over this, and I think I can provide a theoretical explanation of natural origin. First of all, due to his impeccable reputation and above-reproach integrity, I think he did see a flying citadel. Of paramount importance is his vast experience as a pilot and being able to discount any accepted aerial phenomenon or craft. But the city he saw in the sky may have been a reflection from a large town. Simplified, the theory is that a huge flattened concentration of clouds, or a thermal heat inversion, produced a parabolic mirror effect: a huge looking glass in the sky. Don Rosendo was at the Biospheric lab at the time, and my calculations would put the town of Ceballos in the wrong direction for his sighting. Also, Ceballos does not contain the types of lights that reminded Don Rosendo of grids of city streetlights. But on the edge of the Zone, approximately forty-five degrees northeast of the Biospheric lab, is the giant chemical plant of Quimica del Rey. Further investigation has shown me that Quimica del Rey is, in fact, a small self-contained town with intense industrial lighting on all its "streets." I believe that Don Rosendo was witnessing a reflection of the plant caused by a quirk of nature, and as the clouds or thermal heat inversion moved, so it might have appeared did the flying city.

Bibliography

Associated Press. Intelligent Life on Other Planets: A poll. New York, September 1985.

Berlitz, Charles. Without a Trace. New York, 1977.

———. The Bermuda Triangle. New York, 1974.

Blosser, John. Zone of Silence. Unpublished, Florida, 1979.

Daniken, Erich Von. Chariots of the Gods. Trans. by Michael Heron, New York, 1970.

———. Gods from Outer Space. Trans. by Michael Heron, New York, 1971.

———. In Search of Ancient Gods. Trans. by Michael Heron, New York, 1974.

Ebon, Martin (Ed.). The Riddle of the Bermuda Triangle. New York, 1972.

Fireman, E.L. Freshly Fallen Meteorites from Portugal and Mexico. Sky and Telescope, pp. 272–275, May 1969.

Green, H.W. II; Radcliffe, S.V.; and Heuer, A.H. Allende Meteorite: A High-Voltage Electron Petrographic Study. Science, Vol. 172, pp. 936–939, May 1971.

Hunt, Gerald L. Incredible Zone of Silence. Unpublished, New York, 1983.

Hynek, J. Allen. The UFO Experience. Chicago, 1972.

Kawalski, Jack M. Mystery of the Allende Meteorite. UFO Update No. 1, Fall 1978.

Krupp, E.C. (Ed.). In Search of Ancient Astronomies. New York, 1978.

Lewis, Roy S.; Srinivasan, B.; and Anders, Edward. Host Phase of a Strange Xenon Component in Allende. Science, Vol. 190, pp. 1251–1270, December 1975.

Maeda, Luis. Laguna Insolita: Un Interesante Estudio. Torreon, Mexico, 1978.

———. Laguna Insolita: Bacterias Fossiles. Torreon, Mexico, 1980.

———. Laguna Insolita: La Tortuga Terrestre Gigante de Mexico. Torreon, Mexico, date unknown.

————. Laguna Insolita: Mutaciones en la Zona del Silencio. Torreon, Mexico, date unknown.

————. Laguna Insolita: Hallazgos Arguelogicos en la Zona del Silencio. Torreon, Mexico, date unknown.

————. Laguna Insolita: Y . . . . . . Que de la Zona del Silencio. Torreon, Mexico, date unknown.

————. Laguna Insolita: El Cono Athena. Torreon, Mexico, date unknown.

————. Laguna Insolita: El Bosque Fosil de Cauca. Torreon, Mexico, date unknown.

Pellegrino, Charles R., and Stoff, Jesse A. Organic Clues in Carbonaceous Meteorites. Sky and Telescope, pp. 330–332, April 1979.

Persinger, Michael A., and Lafreniere, Gyslaine F. Space-Time Transients and Unusual Events. Chicago, 1977.

Project Blue Book: Official UFO Drawings and Descriptions. Date unknown, obtained under the Freedom of Information Act, Secretary of the Air Force, New York City.

Rancitelli, L.A.; Perkins, R.W.; and Cooper, J.A., et al. Radionuclide Composition of the Allende Meteorite from Nondestructive Gamma-Ray Spectrometric Analysis. Science, Vol. 166, pp. 1269–1271, December 1969.

Sagan, Carl. Intelligent Life in the Universe. San Francisco, 1966.

Scientific American. Protostuff: The Allende Meteorite. Vol. 225, No. 2, p. 42, 1971.

Seitz, M.G., and Kushiro, I. Melting Relations of the Allende Meteorite. Science, Vol. 181, pp. 954–956, March 1974.

Smith, Piers P.K., and Buseck, Peter R. Graphitic Carbon in the Allende Meteorite: A Microstructural Study. Science, Vol. 212, pp. 322–324, April 1981.

Stirling, Mathew W. Mexico's Great Stone Spheres. National Geographic, pp. 295–300, August 1969.

Winer, Richard. The Devil's Triangle 2. New York, 1975.

SPECIFIC NEWS PUBLICATIONS

Correo del Parral, Mexico, 1969.

El Siglo de Torreon, Mexico, 1979–1986.

National Enquirer, 1969 and 1983.

News World. Zone of Silence. New York, December 12, 1981.

Waco Dispatch-Press. Mexican Devil's Triangle Discovered. February 4, 1977.

For further information on curiosities from the Zone, please write to: "Zone," Northern News Service International Inc., 268 Ball Pond Road, New Fairfield, Connecticut 06812.